The Western Gods

by Caleb Eatough

Dedicated to Dante

"There are two rules whereby we are to walk one towards another: Justice and Mercy."

-John Winthrop, *A Modell of Christian Charity*

Prologue

The great coyote padded silently across the desolate prairie. Silver moonlight shone from his searching eyes.

The wind stirred his mangy fur. He snapped at the wind, swatted at it with a bearlike paw, raised his nose to catch the scent. The coyote cackled, his lonely cry echoing off the mountain peaks. He trotted toward a dry stream bed from whence the cloying smell came.

A woman cradled a man's head in her lap. Her golden hair and white buffalo skin shone with the moon's color. Her tears left shining marks on the man's face. It seemed as if he was asleep. He held a great silver bow across his chest, his grip undiminished in the cold rictus of death.

The coyote crouched, watching the woman with longing eyes. When she did finally notice him, she looked at him directly, unafraid. "How many more will you devour, Coyote? When there are so few of us left already?"

The coyote cackled again. The woman drew herself up, dusted off the dirt of the Great Plains. "The winds are changing. You would do well to realize that. If you continue on this path, soon you will be alone. Then what will you do? Will you be content to fade away?"

She took the bow, and a branch from the ground. "You cannot have these."

The moon flashed, blinding the coyote. In the place of the woman stood a great white buffalo. It tossed its head. The coyote scampered away, only to circle back downwind after the buffalo had gone. He devoured the man, laughing, tears spilling from his radiant yellow eyes.

He sniffed the air once more. A new scent, and new prey.

Chapter 1

"Here and there I travel, but everywhere, I walk alone. The closer I get, the farther I go. I fall, but I never reach the bottom. I rise but never touch the sky. Where am I? What am I doing here?"

I found myself at the edge of a dark wood. I traipsed along the bleached road. Stalks of corn listened to the moaning trees. I raised my hand to the phantom fingers of sweet lupine caressing my cheek, as an amputee to his stump.

I heard something behind me.

The empty miles stared back at me.

Turning back to the trail, I saw a young woman in the cornfields, staring at me, laughing. Bloodred hair. And naked.

I blinked. She vanished.

What sinful thoughts had conjured this apparition?

The west wind whistled in my ears, tossed my long red mane. My land called to me. I once danced in its radiant love. But it has grown cold. The leaves are falling. I do not know if they will grow back this time.

I watched him pace from place to place, but he always walked alone. I stalked him through my beloved fields, under the poppy sky. My prey. Both of us purposeless and alone.

In a seedy saloon in Fort Lyon, I pondered my next step, playing with the small golden cross about my neck.

The greasy bartender slapped his rag on the counter. "Whaddaya want?"

I cleared my throat and put away the cross. "Just water, thank you."

A barstool groaned beside me. "Not a drinker, eh, young'un?" A lanky, gray-bearded man chewed on his tobacco. He clapped me on the back. I shied away from the touch.

"No. I am a priest."

"That matters?" He extended his hand. "Welcome to Fort Lyon, padre. Though you are so young, I doubt you could be anyone's padre."

"Alan Cormac."

"I am Brand. Where you been and where you bound?"

What an odd name. "I walked from New York to convert the Indian tribes."

"I thought you looked roadworn. Any news?"

I shrugged. "Any news I have is outdated. It took me a long time to get here. I was on my way to Bent's Fort."

"The Bent brothers burned that down years ago. Cholera. This one is his new one."

I closed my eyes and shook my head. "I had a cousin living there." I needed him so I could plan my next steps. I did not know much about the Indians in Colorado, only that I was called to serve here. My cousin and I had planned this out carefully. He was the one who knew the Indians' ways, not me. But how had he sent the letter if the fort had burned down years ago? Evidently, we had not planned carefully enough.

"So, anything new going on?"

I resisted my urge to retort. He apparently needed something to talk about. A sudden vision of the man's soul, tossed about like an autumn leaf, fluttering above an endless chasm, flashed before my eyes. It could be a chance to save a soul. "President Lincoln emancipated the slaves. I am sure you have heard of that by now. The Civil War continues. The Union took Vicksburg when I set out from New York. It seems the North is finally turning the tables on the secessionists."

Brand scratched his beard. "What is his name?"

"Who?"

"Your cousin."

Thrown by the sudden change in topic, I glanced at him. His stare flashed, like an animal caught in bright moonlight. "Angus."

"I think I remember it. Yep, I remember him. Went and married a Cherokee woman six months back. Probably living in some godforsaken hole in the mountains by now. How long has he been living out here?"

I pulled out the letter. "About nine months. The letter is dated only four months ago."

"Well, I am going thataway tomorrow if you want to survey the ruins. Only a few hours to the west. You can be there and back by nightfall."

What else could I do? "Most kind of you, Brand."

Brand's wagon took up most of the road. The wide open plains left room for the wind to scurry. The mountains loomed in the distance, far larger than the Appalachians. Like the maw of a bear.

He pointed the fort out to me. "The Bents set it up as a trading post with the Indians, Cheyenne and Arapaho mostly, a few Navajo. Most of the buildings are still standing, not livable though."

We came to a fork in the road. I clambered out of the wagon. "Thank you again, Brand. God remembers these acts of kindness."

"Figgered I would be blessed if I helped a saint." He grinned. His teeth reminded me of a rabid coyote I had seen during my travels.

"Priest."

"Holy man. Whatever."

Perhaps the people out here needed God as much as the savages.

I walked the rest of the way to the fort. A bend in the Arkansas River hugged the hill, which sported a few scraggly trees. The Great Plains stretched the vast wilderness beyond. The fort itself was quite large. It had been a major outpost, not the shack I had expected, though nothing compared to sprawling New York, either.

I reached the scorched stucco walls. The gate had collapsed. Beyond that, I could see several of the buildings had caved in. I prayed for the lives lost to cholera, then climbed over the wreckage.

Everything was stained with soot. What was not broken or burned had been looted thrice over. A dried carcass, picked by vultures.

I heard something shuffling in the doorway of a still-intact building. The hairs stood up on the back of my neck, but I peered inside. Something vaguely human-shaped squatted in the darkness. Pain coursed through my head. I collapsed.

Shadows played in front of my eyelids. Voices around me. Was that father? I was so sleepy, but he was not reciting the Lord's Prayer…

I remembered through a haze of pain. The fort. I tried to feel the bump on my head, but I could not move my hands. Rough bark scratched my back through my clothes. A knot on my head swelled to what felt like the size of a lemon. I closed my eyes. Nauseating.

"Water."

I opened my eyes, and then wished I had not. Night had fallen. A weathered man dressed in homespun cloth crouched before me, a fire highlighting his outline. He held a small pouch to my lips. I tried to take it, but my hands strained against tight leather bonds. Such indignity. If I had not been bound I would have…

My lips cracked. I sipped hesitantly. The water was cool and earthy.

Once I was finished, he placed a gag over my mouth. The savage, for he was obviously Indian, nodded in satisfaction and proceeded back to his fire, where ten more of his kind sat talking. Some pawed through the loot they had taken from the area. Pots and pans, a gun or two, some food, even a saddled horse tied to a tree. More horses stood beyond the firelight's edge. I could not tell what the savages said, but they were happy and expansive.

Nobody would come looking for me. I could not talk my way out of here, not unless their vocabulary extended beyond "water" and "food." I looked about for a sharp rock, something I could use to cut my bonds. They had bound my ankles as well. I prayed to Jesus. I did not know what they wanted with me, and I did not want to.

Exhaustion and nausea overcame me once more. I laid my head against the tree trunk, head spinning with useless plans.

I woke up with a nose in my ear. "Mmmmmfff!" The gag was still in my mouth. The embers glowing softly in the savage's fire pit blinded me.

A slender finger replaced the nose despite my muffled protests. Warm, honeyed breath fanned over my neck and hair. It smelled flowery…like lupine. Were these people so much like animals?

"Hmmm."

The breath over my hands felt like a warm summer's breeze. This person was sniffing my bonds. The savage shuffled on bare feet to my ankles. "Hmmm."

She was a woman. Would a raiding party bring a woman along?

Something furry brushed my face. Exploratory hands touched my ankles, my legs, my stomach. I twitched. The hands ignored me and continued to my face, where they found my gag. "Ah."

She tore off the gag. The light of the embers traced her vague outline. Her head was cocked to one side, like a frolicsome fox. She pressed a finger to my lips. "Be quiet."

"Who are you?"

"Shush. They have a guard, and his ears are sharp."

She certainly did not talk like a savage. A vaguely familiar accent. It conjured childhood memories. And a strange stirring, deep in my insides.

The strange woman untied my hands and ankles. "Can you stand?"

I stood, and nausea flooded through me. I staggered against the tree. Her bare arms caught me.

"Lean on me," she ordered. "Step quietly."

I put my arm around her shoulders. Her naked shoulders. "Are you—?"

"Quiet!" She hushed me with another finger. We awkwardly crept through the brush. I strained to hear anything from my captors, but my pounding heart drowned out their snores.

I heard a yelp, and a yell from the campsite. "Pla'ar do theach." My companion sighed, as if she had been caught in a game of tag. "Run!"

We stumbled over logs. Branches whipped my face.

"What's wrong with you?"

"I cannot see!"

"Of all the...take my hand!"

The path grew easier, but our pursuers had torches. "They found our trail," my rescuer said. "Of course they did, you blundering about like that. Left one wide as a buffalo for them."

"I beg your pardon? I'm no woodsman!" I was from New York, not the godforsaken wilderness! But my prayer had been answered. I had been saved!

She snorted, but her feet, sure as a goat's, pattered a fast path through the brush. We broke from the sparse trees, dashing into an open field. My heart pumped, my knees wobbled, but my rescuer pulled me onward. The flickering light of a torch appeared in the woods before us. We dashed left, but another flame blocked our path. We turned to the right, but a savage waited for us. He could not see us yet, but he moved purposefully. We turned back the way we came.

An Indian brandishing his torch charged at us. My rescuer leaped into the torchlight, hissing like a demented animal. He froze comically in mid-stride, eyes wide and staring, mouth open. "Yei Naadlooshii!" he screeched. He dropped his torch and fled.

The dry grass caught fire. My rescuer stamped out the fire with a bare foot, but not before I saw...something.

She was completely naked. She had red hair...and was that a... tail? Or had her backside caught fire?

I blinked. Darkness shrouded us once more. Our pursuers had fled. They probably had the right idea. My head pounded, my eyes felt like lumps of lard. I fell forward.

Her soft arms caught me. She murmured, "Poor fool. Completely exhausted. There now, sleep." Her hand pressed on my forehead. "Sleep, my prey."

An overwhelming compulsion hung lead weights on my eyelids. For the third time, I fell unconscious.

Sunlight, and a blinding headache, awoke me. I groaned, rolling over stiffly to a face two inches from mine. "Sleep well?"

Last night leaped into my mind like a fox into a chicken house. Staring at me with large gray eyes, her chin resting on the top of her hands, was my rescuer. Her hair swept the ground in red tangles. She grinned at me, revealing abnormally long canines.

"I asked you a question."

I averted my eyes. How could she look so comfortable, naked, her belly on the ground? Had she no modesty? Perhaps not. If she was a savage, she would not have been taught about such things. A verse popped into my head. *And they were naked, and were not ashamed.* Yes, she was certainly that.

"Did the blow to your head rattle all the words around? Or has the fox got your tongue?"

She rolled her r's faintly, purring. Her odd speech briefly overcame my shyness. "Is it not 'cat'?"

Those large, luminous gray eyes and crooked smile pinned me like a hypnotized rat. "I prefer foxes."

"Who are you?"

She cackled, sitting up. I averted my eyes again.

"What's wrong with you?"

"You are naked."

"What of it?"

"I am a priest."

"What of that?"

"Where are your clothes?"

She smirked. "I have none."

"Did the Indians take them?"

"I have never worn clothes."

Her strange reply overcame my sinful thoughts. I stared. "Even the Indians wear clothes. What is your name, miss?"

"Eithne."

No surname? "Where do you hail from, Miss Eithne?"

"Hail?" Her brows furrowed, and she bit her lower lip. It was…endearing. My face grew hot again, and I looked down at my shaking hands. "I don't hail from anywhere. Or, perhaps I hail from everywhere. The earth is my home. Look at me," she snapped. "You're acting shamed, and it's irritating."

"I am protecting your decency," I said, though I was not sure why I bothered, as she had no interest in protecting it herself.

"Oh, very well." She snapped her fingers.

"You may take my coat—"I began, but a new sight sent fresh waves of bafflement.

A fox padded up beside her, carrying a blanket in its teeth. I stared at it. Suspicion crawled up my spine.

"You may look now, squeamish one."

I kept my face averted. What spells might she cast on me? "Have you consorted with demons?" I had heard of wild stories of demon-possessed savages, but I had never given the stories much credence until now.

She took my chin in her hand. A soft, small hand, but very strong. The blanket now covered her enough so I could look at her without shame. She wore it like a queen, though she was very young. About seventeen. "The Dineh called me something like it…Skinwalker. Hunter of men. Demon I am not. Hunter, I am."

She frowned. "What are you?" Still gripping my chin, she turned my face, examining me. "I thought I knew. You have that smell about you, like ripe blueberries. But you're human."

Gathering my courage, I clenched my teeth and squared my shoulders. "I am a follower of the Lord Jesus Christ. Begone, demon, in the name of Jesus."

She looked puzzled, rather than terrified as I had hoped. "You look ridiculous with your hackles raised. Deflate yourself. Who is this Jesus you speak of?"

Very well. My ministry would begin with her. "He is God."

"What kind of god?"

The demon-possessed would not ask such questions, but an angel would know his Lord. "He is God. The God. The almighty God, who came down in the flesh and saved us all from sin."

Her head tilted in that same gesture of curiosity I had seen the night before. "So...you are a priest of this god? Have you come upon my lands to proselytize?"

"I have." I processed her reply again. "Your lands?"

"Yes. My lands. I am this land's caretaker."

Unease, and pity, crept into my bowels. She was obviously deranged from living in the wilderness too long. I could see she was no savage, not with the red hair and accent, which I still could not quite place. "What are you, then?"

The crooked smile appeared once more. She stretched luxuriously. "I am Eithne, goddess of the three sisters."

"The three what?"

"The three sisters!"

"Excuse me. I have no idea what you are on about."

She blew a lock of hair away from her face. "Maize, beans, and squash."

So, this man was a priest, not the god himself. My nose had been mistaken.

I had heard of some gods lending their powers to mortals. Mostly the ones interested in worship. Only a priest. Not worth outsmarting…or eating.

I looked him up and down again. I could tell whether someone threw lightning, or controlled the weather. His blessing evaded me. Why did the Dineh want this milkish pup? They rarely ventured beyond their lands because of some ridiculous superstition. But they had come this far, and found this man.

The poor fool's eyes jittered in their sockets. All males were the same. So he was a virtuous priest...or attempting to be. He hadn't handled his trappers well.

"Corn and…squash?"

And I had to keep repeating things for him, too. "Yes, and don't forget the beans," I responded patiently. "Why has this Jesus not faced me himself, priest?" The name of his god…it pricked hazy, distorted memories, like a cloud of dandelion seeds. Itchy.

"Jesus wants us to have faith."

"An invisible god then. What is his territory?"

"The world is his domain. He created it."

I scratched my ear. "What is your name?"

"Cormac. Alan Cormac."

"Have you ever heard of me?"

"I have not."

"There, see?"

"See what?"

"Gods who want worship want attention. You haven't heard of me. That means I'm a proper goddess. I am no demon, nor have I consorted with any. So stop thinking about such things."

I could almost see the light of understanding brighten his eyes. He looked like he wanted to ask another question, but instead he said, "Thank you for saving me. I would like to go back to Fort Lyon now and have a doctor examine the bump on my head."

"Do as you wish." A man of faith, unwilling to believe. How amusing.

I watched him stagger to the river, wash his face, take a drink, then set off stiffly. "Ah...priest. Your town is the other way."

He looked back at me, then in the direction I pointed. "So it is. Thank you, once again."

Poor hopeless man. He was like a mountain goat which had picked a fight with a stone. Dazed and confused.

I stalked him up the allspice-road. It wouldn't do for my prey to fall into another's trap.

What had just happened? She had just been there, and then...gone. Vanished.

Perhaps I had imagined her. But, how would I have escaped by myself?

It seemed absurd. Surely I had dreamed it. I had hit my head, and dreamed of a naked woman.

I confessed this sin to God as I walked back to Fort Lyon. My stomach growled and my feet dragged when I finally arrived at the fort that evening. The autumn wind bit at my unprotected head. People gave me sidelong looks. I glanced down at myself. I looked as haggard as I felt. My clothes were dirt-stained and rumpled, and my black hair shed layers of dust.

I dug out my paltry change and sighed. My journey had begun with a much larger sum. I could not continue much longer unless I found a job or learned how to feed off the wilderness. I had not expected my goal to be in jeopardy before it began.

I had no other choice. I rented a room in the saloon I had stayed in the night before last, washed, then took a meal by the fireplace. Trusting in God had become my last option. I shook my head. If he could forgive even my sins, He could also grant my wish. I had not done much to inspire His confidence, however. If anything, I deserved divine retribution.

Someone interrupted my thoughts. "So, you lived then."

I jumped. It took me a moment to recognize Brand. "What do you mean?"

"Figgered I would check in on you on my way back, see if you needed a ride, or if you had found your cousin. You are new here, so I felt a little responsible." He grinned, planting himself in an adjacent chair, revealing yellowed, pointed teeth. "I saw markings of a scuffle. Some Injuns attack you?"

"I…I suppose they did." I had not been dreaming that part, then. This man was very kind, despite his roguish exterior. Most people I had met from New York to here would not take trouble for a stranger. "Right when I entered the fort. They hit me on the head and tied me to a tree. I woke up at nightfall, only a few yards away from the fort wall." The details of the night became sharper after some recovery. "It seemed odd that they did not run after catching me."

"Raids have been happening for the last week or so. About ten adventuresome Injuns. They must have wanted to raid another homestead before setting off. Lawkeeper thinks they are Navajo, but it's a long way from the South. How did you escape?"

What would I tell him? That a corn goddess had spirited me away? My conscience shied from lying to him, but the night had been confusing to me as well. Best to avoid complications. "I do not know. I seem to remember a woman leading me. I remember them coming after us…one of them screamed something, and then they all disappeared. I fainted, and this morning I woke up and came here."

"What did he yell? You remember?"

"I think…yes…it was 'yee naldooshi,' or something like it."

Brand leaned back in his chair, balancing on the back legs. "Yei naadlooshii." Squinting at me, he said, "They are Navajo, alright. That word means 'skinwalker.' It is a legend about animals who can change into people. They are hunters, like, man-hunters. Summat must have spooked them."

My neck hairs prickled at this explanation.

Brand patted me on the shoulder and stood up. "I better go tell this to the people who can do something about it.

Expect some lawman to come about and question you tomorrow. Take care of yourself." He ambled dustily out of the inn.

What would I tell them? The only details I really remembered were the ones about the girl!

I stifled my imagination. My treacherous mind flashed images of her until I finally suppressed my lecherous thoughts with an overwhelming desire for sleep.

I hefted myself from my chair, the soft bed upstairs calling to my aching limbs.

My prey had momentarily evaded me, but I found his scent and followed it to a communal den at the center of their gathering place. Humans are so…unnatural. Using fire to warm their dens? It seems almost arrogant. Prometheus had given them fire, so they could cook meat and warm themselves. I look at it not as a source of warmth but of cleansing, to renew the soil. Fire was a tool of the gods.

From what I had seen of humans, they had many inventive uses for fire, not all of them savory. I eyed the flickering flames as I stared at my priest from outside. He talked with an old man who seemed concerned for him. They weren't related. They weren't friends, either. The old one looked more like he wanted to eat him.

Their conversation ended. The man came out of the den. He seemed familiar, somehow. A memory tugged at me through the dark, tangled woods of my past. Perhaps I had known one of his ancestors?

My thoughts scattered like the autumn leaves when he addressed me. "Miss? You look a little lost."

I regained my composure and looked him in the eye. "I was just looking for a friend. He's a…man of Jesus."

"There are one or two around here. What is his name?"

"Cormac."

"You are in luck, I just finished talking to him. He is staying here."

"Thank you." Why did this man look so familiar? My memory lapses were starting to worry me.

I swept past him into the communal den. The priest stood by the fire, yawning. Picking my way through the scattered stick-legged flat eating things and square-sitting things, I stalked behind him. "Did you miss me, holy one?"

He started like a ruffled chicken. "Good Lord!" Then he recognized me, and a cloud fell over him. "I was not hallucinating then. Was I?"

"Why would you think so in the first place?" I slid into the square sitting-place opposite his. By my action, I hoped to pressure him to sit down. He did so, reluctantly, and I smiled in triumph.

"I see you have managed to procure clothing, Miss Eithne."

"Do you like it?" I preened, running my hands over my luxurious parsley-green cloak. I couldn't hear quite as well with the hood, but that was a small price to pay for such a nice garment. I wore a fine silk shirt and short allspice-brown dress. I loved turning my gray eyes different colors with this clothing. Right now, they reflected the green and brown, and the fire would set the colors dancing. My prey looked grudgingly appreciative.

"Where did you procure them?"

"Oh, here and there."

He raised an eyebrow. "You stole them?"

Hah. Not nearly the reaction I expected. "Everything a goddess needs is given to her." I eyed the remains of his food. "Are you still hungry?"

"No." Curt, dismissive. I ignored his tone. For now.

"Thirsty maybe?"

"No."

"Do they have chicken here?"

"I do not know."

"You lie. I smell them. How could you not smell them?"

Someone began banging on the instrument in the corner. "What is that called?" I pointed to it.

He looked puzzled. "A piano."

"It's very noisy. I'm going to stop it." I got up out of my squeaking sitting-thing and glided toward the den-keeper.

By the Lord above, she had followed me!

Before I could stop her, she had gone off to stop the piano. Contrary to what I expected, she went straight for the innkeeper. The innkeeper creaked over the counter in light conversation with the pianist. Eithne asked him something, presumably about the chicken. He nodded and went back to the kitchen. She leaned on the counter, looking –I was sure it was an act— quite innocent and vulnerable.

The saloon's patrons had increased. Presently, a hulking cowboy swaggered up to her. He leaned next to her, obviously drunk, and said something. She responded, smiling shyly. The cowboy made a suggestion, and a gesture upstairs. Eithne looked offended, and shook her head. Laying a hand on her forearm, he leered at her.

I stood, about to help her. The cowboy dragged her past the piano toward the stairs. He tripped. Eithne slipped out of his grip. He barreled into the piano player, sending them both sprawling to the floor.

Everyone in the saloon looked up at the clatter. "Sorry," she said with a demure smile, covering her mouth in embarrassment. "So very sorry. I'll just…"

With the perfect act of a mockingjay, she scurried back to my table. When the patrons went back to eating and conversation, she smiled wickedly.

"You may want to be more careful about things like that. That man could have done anything he wanted to you if you had not tripped him."

"I didn't trip him; the noisemaker did."

"And what if he had not?"

She waved her hand dismissively. "I would have found another way to trip him."

"Things could have become violent. That man had only one thing on his mind. Something very unsavory."

Eithne cocked her head. "What did he have on his mind, priest?"

I stared at her. How she could be so uncaring, so frivolous and ignorant…well. The verse came to me again. *They were naked, and they were not ashamed.* She seemed…untainted. Innocent. A strange impression, given the encounter, but it remained like a burr in my shoe. "Never mind."

We sat in silence. Eithne kept sniffing the air, presumably for the chicken. I stewed, trying to make my tired mind discern an escape path. I thought of several schemes, each one wilder than the last. Fleeing home might not be such a bad idea after all.

As I was about to do so, I noticed Eithne staring at me. Her eyes did not gleam with mischief this time.

"Where did you come from, priest of Jesus?"

The question was unexpected, and I jittered my reply. "I…I came from New York."

"Where is that?"

"Many miles east and north of here, on the Atlantic Ocean."

"Ah. So you have come very far."

"Yes…very far. Especially if you walk."

Eithne studied me for a long time. She seemed to be looking at my soul through my eyes. "You walked here all the way from New York. Yet you mewl like a pup when you stray off the path." She grinned, but something else lurked behind her grin.

I bristled. She waved her hand. "Don't puff up like that. I was complimenting you."

It did not seem like a compliment, but I decided not to argue. We sat in more genial silence until the innkeeper brought out a steaming plate.

"Are you truly planning to eat all of that?" I stared pointedly at the whole chicken permeating the air with a pleasant aroma.

"Of course!" Eithne looked up at the keeper. "You can put the cost on this man's…tab. He's a priest, and he offered to pay for me."

"A very generous man," the man said as he looked at me for his money. I made strangling noises. The words running through my head were very impolite.

Chapter 2

Her manners had scandalized me.

My mother's chicken tasted better anyway, and I said so to Miss Eithne. When I went to bed, I expected to sleep soundly, despite the carnage of chicken I had witnessed. However, the whole night, I felt eyes on me. It reminded me of when that rabid coyote had stalked me on the road. I had not known it had been there until yellow eyes flashed in the brush. I ran very far, very fast, to evade that monstrosity.

When I made it downstairs at about ten o'clock, two men waited for me. One, grizzled and old in a battered brown hat, introduced himself as the sheriff. The other, younger, clean-shaven and dapper, his deputy.

"We have some questions for you. Do you have some time?" The sheriff shook my hand politely and gestured for me to sit at a table. Both of them sat down across from me, the chairs squeaking on the worn wood floor.

"I am Richard Pierce. Now, I would like to hear about what went on between you and the Injuns yesterday."

I told him the same story I had told Brand. They seemed impressed. "Could you give any more detail on who rescued you? She was not with them, was she?"

I started to sweat. "No. I mean, it was dark and I could not tell—"

"It was me."

All three of our heads swiveled to stare at Eithne, who had just come in the front door. "I rescued him."

Pierce tipped his hat to Eithne. Despite her diminutive size, something about her eyes made one think she could run off a herd of buffalo. "Do you have anything useful to add, miss?"

Eithne tapped her chin, thoughtful. I eyed her warily. "They were Dineh. They have horses, so you're not going to catch them. And last time I saw them, they were fleeing back South."

"Fleeing?"

Eithne smiled, tight-lipped. "Did I say fleeing?"

"Do you mind telling us how you know that?"

"I kept an eye on them. The homesteaders told me when they saw them. They didn't bother hiding themselves." Smooth lie. If indeed it was a lie. I could be sure of nothing with this girl.

"Still, they're only a day out," The deputy whispered to Pierce. "They could turn right back around today."

"Just who exactly are you, miss? I have not seen you around these parts before."

"Oh, I've lived out here for *ages*."

"I think we have given the good sheriff all of the information we can give," I interrupted, shooting a warning glance at Eithne. "It would be uncharitable of us to take up any more of his time."

"Thank you for your information, Mr. Cormac." Pierce stood up and shook my hand. "I better go see what I can do to keep these Injuns from coming back."

He and his deputy left the saloon. I turned to Eithne. "If you start telling people you are a goddess, they may take it into their heads to burn you for a witch," I said. Bluntness may work where courtesy failed, I reasoned.

She only grinned. I tried again. "Are you worried at all?"

"Do you not believe in witches?"

I blinked, making the mistake of looking into her hypnotic eyes. "I do. At least, I think I do."

"I assure you, I'm not a witch. Decide if you believe in them or not. Whether you truly believe matters little to me." She looked me up and down. "But I hate indecisiveness."

I gritted my teeth. "That was quite out of line."

She shrugged. Perhaps she was not possessed by demons, but she was possessed of an inexhaustible desire to annoy me.

"How did you know they were going to question me?"

Eithne flipped a stray lock of hair back into her hood. "You didn't mind me helping you, did you?"

She laughed at my expression. "I thought so! You're not a very good liar, are you?"

"*I* do not make a habit of it." I was wasting time here.

"Where are you going?"

"To the mountains," I answered.

"To the Arapaho? They can be more violent than the Dineh!"

"If you are a goddess," I said as I began to leave the room, "why do you care?"

She cocked her head. "Is your Jesus a jealous god?"

"In a manner of speaking." I turned my back on her.

When I came back down, she had gone. I put her out of my head. I had enough to deal with without worrying about a deranged woman.

It was a good thing I had not taken most of my belongings with me, else they would be heading toward Mexico with the Navajo. Of the things I had taken with me to Bent's Fort, I had been most fortunate to keep my gold Celtic cross I hung about my neck. The rest, not counting my clothes, had been absconded with, to my deep displeasure.

I had been on the road for several hours. The evening sun warmed me nearly past endurance, despite winter's nip in the air. One moment the sky would be perfectly clear, the next, a rainstorm would be filling up my boots. But on the whole it shone more than it rained, and the air was always dry.

I set down my rucksack next to a solitary boulder. Shading my eyes, taking a bite of bread, I stared at the mountains. They filled me with awe. The Cascades were mere bumps by comparison, gums compared with the white-tipped teeth of the Rockies.

I took a deep breath. The air, sweet with the smell of freedom, stirred restlessly. It whispered a question in my ear. "What are you running from?"

With a sigh I turned, and met a pair of gray, soulful eyes. "What are you running from?" she asked again.

"What--" I tripped, sprawled. "Oh," I said, shaking my head. "It's you."

"I know it's me. I asked you a question."

"I do not have to answer. Go home. Leave me in peace."

I picked up my rucksack and started down the road once more. She scurried to reach my side. "I can help you."

"Help me with what?"

"I know their language. And I know you don't."

I eyed her suspiciously. "What will you want in return?"

"Only the satisfaction of my curiosity."

She lifted her nose to the air. Smelling out my secrets. All the while, her eyes darted back and forth, looking at every scrub of grass or darting mouse. "You seemed in quite a hurry. What were you running from?"

"What, did you follow me from New York?"

"No. Just from the lake-river."

Lake-river? "Would that be the Mississippi?"

"I don't know what it's called in your tongue."

"You should keep track of your languages. Especially if you wish to be my translator."

"I am speaking your tongue."

"Yes, English, but 'Mississippi' is Indian. And what kind of accent is that?"

She chewed on a fingernail absently, still gazing about. "I don't know." She frowned.

Having successfully diverted her probe into my past, I returned to the road. A perfunctory tap on my shoulder distracted me again. "Aren't you afraid?"

"Of what?"

"Of being alone."

I sighed. "I will not be free of you, will I?"

She grinned. "No."

"Very well. You may come along if you wish."

"Don't worry, priest. I will keep my promise."

I grunted. I was not being a gentleman, or charitable, but at the moment I did not care.

I suddenly noticed a weight missing from my neck. She dangled my cross in front of my nose. I held out my hand. "Please give my cross back."

"But I like it."

I shook my head. She fell into step beside me. "I'll give it back."

I grunted again. A hawk called, then dived for a rodent. "Are priests of Jesus suicidal?" She sniffed at the cross. With a longsuffering air, I tried to ignore her. "That will be the outcome," she continued, "if you go without the protection of your god."

She dangled my cross in front of me like a trainer dangling a carrot in front of a horse. "Objects carry no power," I said.

"I know."

"What are you about then?" Where once I could not look at her, now I could not take my eyes off her. Did she know? But how could she know?

Shaking off my private shame, I attempted to snatch my cross from her. She danced out of reach. "Please give it back," I said again.

"I will."

"It is a trinket. Worthless."

"It's valuable to you. I will give it back, priest. When I'm finished with it."

"Very well," I said shortly. "Do what you will."

We set out northwest toward Denver the next day. The journey would take two and a half days. The road was hot and dusty, like it had been on my trip here. I could do without the heat. In New York, the ocean carried away most of it, but here it baked the land like crackers in an oven.

I could not reconcile my thoughts. I, a good Christian, and a priest, was traveling in the company of a…demon possessed girl. A girl of few virtues. It seemed contradictory, yet it was the only opportunity I could take to accomplish my dream. I did need a translator. God provided, but He had a sense of humor as well.

She had slept some distance from me. At least, that is what I assumed, given that I saw neither hide nor hair of her until late afternoon.

As I suffered in the early autumn heat, Eithne frolicked in the tall grass lining the road. She flowed through it like the wind. I detected no trace of the ancient goddess she claimed to be. Not possessed either. More like an innocent girl.

"Isn't it glorious?" She twirled, and before I could catch her, flopped in the dirt.

Shocked, I kneeled at her side. "Are you all right?"

Turning herself over, she giggled. "I'm well!" Leaping to her feet, she skipped away, humming tunelessly. "I love this time of year."

I dusted my pants off. "Why do I bother?" I muttered.

She danced ahead of me until I could no longer hear her humming, disappearing for a time.

When I saw her next, it was nearly evening, and she was curled up by the side of the road. I moved to see if she had somehow injured herself. A faint snore escaped.

"Why me?" I asked the waning day.

She stirred, blinking. "Oh, my," she said, with no hint of embarrassment. "I seem to have fallen asleep." She stretched her arms toward me. "Carry me."

My jaw worked as I thought of something to say. If this was what it would be like with her as a travelling companion…

"Can you stand?"

"I'm tired."

"You were frolicsome enough earlier."

"I was excited earlier."

"Did you sleep last night?"

"No."

My face fell into my hand. She stuck her lip out. "It's hard for me to sleep at night."

I wanted to laugh; at the same time, I wanted to walk past her, and never look back. "Gods need sleep?"

"Hmph. Don't mock me, priest."

I held out my hand. I pulled her up, and we continued down the road.

"We will spend the night here." The sparse plains offered little in the way of shelter or firewood save for a solitary pine.

"Sounds good to me." Eithne yawned. It would have been less annoying had she not yawned in my ear. "Thank you for carrying me."

"You should have slept last night."

"I didn't really think about it."

"You said you would be able to walk alone."

"I said I could walk. I didn't say I could do it alone."

"So that is how I ended up carrying you for two miles." I dumped her unceremoniously in the grass under the lone tree. "Allow me to clarify things. I am eager to help when the occasion demands it. But you are taking advantage of me, and it is starting to get on my nerves."

"I thank you for all of it, don't I?"

I lost my temper then. "That is not the point!"

For once, Eithne's features grew serious and speculative. "I always repay my debts, priest. Remember that I am taking care of our food."

"I have been meaning to ask you about that. You procured bread. Bread! And salted meat. From nowhere. I cannot help but think you stole it! Unless you can conjure it up from nothing."

"I can't 'conjure things up,' and I don't steal!" She pouted. "All I need is given to me. That's the way it has always been."

"Where did you get it from, then?"

"My foxes bring it to me, sometimes."

"And where do they get it?"

"I don't know."

My shoulders slumped. "I am going to sleep. I am too tired to eat anything. Do you want a fire?"

"No. The night seems warm enough."

"Very well."

I spread out my bedroll and sank into it, dreaming of home within a few minutes.

This priest was rather amusing. If I hadn't smelled it, however, I wouldn't have believed him to be a man of power. His god, Jesus, sounded very familiar. As if I had known someone by that name a long time ago. Perhaps I had known this god in my childhood. If so, chasing down that memory would be useless. I had no memory of my childhood. Every god was like that. Perhaps we never had childhoods, but sprung up from the ground when the ground had need of us.

The night was colder than I had thought.

I looked up at the twinkling stars. Once, the gods had been as numerous as those stars. I remembered so many from when I had been younger, living with Mother in the potato fields. Now the blackness swallowed up each pulsing light. I felt like a lone candle in the middle of that vast darkness.

Where did you all go? Why did you leave me here?

I shivered. I had been cold before, but I had never felt it so…acutely. And what was this feeling in my chest? This slow, dull ache, this emptiness? As if my heart were suffering from blight…

The morning greeted me cheerily as I woke up, groggily flailing in the tangled blankets. I had not slept well, though I had slept deeply. Dwelling on my home did that to me. At least I had been warm.

Very warm.

Two arms snaked around my chest. I had gone to bed fully dressed, but it was still enough to scatter my thoughts. "Eithne!"

"What?" She mewled, still half asleep. For a brief instant, she looked incredibly beautiful, with the morning sun shining on her red hair and in her gray eyes. I caught a whiff of lupine. Then she smiled, and I remembered who she was again.

"What are you doing?"

"Eh?" She blinked, then studied our position. "I was cold."

"You act a lot more like a child than a goddess."

"I can get cold as well. I shiver in the cold. I don't like it when I shiver."

I sighed. "Please get out."

Eithne grumpily shoved herself out of my bedroll. Fortunately, she had remembered clothes.

"I offered you some blankets, you know."

"Blankets couldn't help with this chill."

Her luminous gray eyes held an indecipherable expression. As if she imagined herself on a vast, dry plain. A confusing feeling crept up into my head. For a moment, I almost believed her absurd story. "Hungry?" I stammered.

The morning was cool and cheery, the road, endless, my goals, unwavering. I even bounced a little as we plodded toward Denver. Despite my situation, I felt renewed. It baffled me.

"Uhm, Eithne."

She glanced at me distractedly. "What?"

"If you are feeling unwell, we can moderate our pace."

She cocked her head. "Unwell?"

"You mentioned you had a chill."

"And?"

"Maybe you are catching something?"

"Hmph. Impossible. Gods cannot catch disease." Her eyes kept darting south.

"Would you please look at me when I talk to you?" Her manners were absolutely atrocious.

Eithne waved her hand at me. "Shush. I'm concentrating."

I had patiently dealt with everything else she had done to me this morning. I had given her a good portion of breakfast because she had complained she was starving. I had waited for thirty minutes for her to get ready to leave. But this was going too far. I whirled and leveled my finger at her. "Now you listen here—"

Quick as lightning, her teeth latched onto my hand. I yelped and jerked back. "What was that for?"

"What do you think?!" she exploded. "I'm trying to concentrate! You keep distracting me!" She stopped, kneading her forehead. "There," she said after a moment. "Finished."

"What were you doing?"

"Causing a small famine."

"A famine?"

"Yes. The ground needs to rest every once in awhile."

"That sounds…heartless."

She gave me a disgusted look. "Better starving a little now than a lot later. If I didn't, the ground would never recover."

We walked in silent moodiness for awhile. I dwelled on what she had said. I sent a silent prayer up to Jesus…in case Eithne really had caused a famine.

Eithne broke our hostile silence. "So…you were concerned about me?"

I grunted. If she wanted to play this game…

"I mean, you were concerned I might be catching a cold?" I noticed out of the corner of my eye that her hands were kneading her shirt collar.

"Any gentleman would be concerned."

"Do you think I…might…be catching something?" She sounded fearful. Not what I had come to expect from her.

"Maybe. Describe it to me."

"It feels like I'm empty inside, like there's a gaping hole where my heart is. For some reason, it eases when I look at…"

"At what?"

"At…the stars."

She looked to the brilliant sunrise. The rays of light softened her hair into a halo. "I suppose," she said at last, "I've always felt this way. I never noticed before."

Her tone was strained. I said nothing, unable to fathom her change in character. Like the mountain wind, she blew from breeze to gale.

Panic fluttered about inside me like an angry chicken. The ache, the terrible ache, wouldn't go away.

This pain made me want to bury myself in a hole. The possibilities opening up to me felt vast, inexorable, like a giant hammer poised above me.

Gods do not feel pain. So why did I feel this? Was I becoming deaf to the whispers of the land?

That thought sent tremors through me, and I recoiled from it.

"Here. Use my handkerchief."

With a start, I realized my cheeks were wet with eye-rain. I took his strip of cloth gruffly, dabbing my eyes.

Gods and goddesses were solitary, unless they needed something. We did not feel the urges humans had.

I cleaned my face with the handkerchief. Alan rubbed the back of his neck. A nervous rabbit. "Are you sure you are well?"

There was something in his face…compassion? "I'm well. Dust in my eyes."

He smiled strangely, bitterly, even self-mockingly. "I…misjudged you, a little."

I blinked, befuddled.

He coughed self-consciously. "Let us be off."

That night we denned under a tree again. The golden plains stretched out around us, and the mountains stood silent vigil over the Western horizon. I listened to the wind, smelled its dry sweetness, gazed at the stars, watched the wilderness.

"What is your god like?"

Alan poked at the fire. Ignoring me. Undaunted, I continued to needle him.

"Have you seen him?"

"He is invisible."

"Has he ever spoken to you?"

He looked at me. I must have said something he didn't like. I stared back. If he wanted to challenge me, I would show him his place. "He hasn't, has he?"

He said nothing, but his glare said everything.

I blinked. "I think I do not believe your god exists."

"And why is that?" His tone was frosty, biting.

"Have I offended you?"

"Yes. You have."

I raised my eyebrows. "I thought a priest would be more understanding."

His face reddened. I continued. "He has never been seen by his priests. He never speaks to you. Why should I believe he exists at all?"

"His disciples saw him. And some priests had visions of him."

"How long ago did his disciples see him?"

"Eighteen hundred years."

"And he hasn't been seen or heard from in all that time."

"He has."

"By the priests, of course. By the alpha-males."

He crossed his arms. I decided it would be better to stop snarling. "How was your god made?"

He eyed me, then decided there was nothing offensive in my question. He began to poke at the coals again. "He was born in the town of Bethlehem, to a virgin."

"What?" I said sharply. "Born?"

"Born to the virgin Mary." He eyed me, bemused.

"Born to a human?" I laughed. How absurd!

"Yes. He was God before he came down and became Man."

My laughter ceased abruptly. "I thought you were telling me how he began. What about before he was born?"

"He never began. He has always existed."

"How…interesting."

"I shall retire now," he said tersely. He wrapped himself in blankets, and soon he snored quietly. I watched the seething coals, and soon fell asleep as well, though the night had just begun.

Run, run, run!

The trees flying past me were unfamiliar, yet it seemed like they knew me. A thousand golden leaves, like tattered souls, swirled about me in the patched moonlight.

Run!

The beating rabbit-thump of my heart. It was so loud, they were sure to hear it!

Log!

I sprawled, cursing in a strange tongue. The villagers moments behind me! That terrible, cloying presence…

I scrambled to my feet, only to collapse again as my ankle betrayed me. The treeline picketed my path like iron bars. I clambered through the tangled wood and limped up the grassy hill. The stars glared down at me, so bright, as if eager to see them kill me. Up this hill lay my salvation.

An arrow zipped past me. I ducked, limped faster. "There's the girl!" Eerie red torchlight behind me.

Another arrow. I collapsed, feeling the searing pain in my other leg! Sobbing, I clutched at handfuls of grass, pulling myself desperately up the hill. "Why have you forsaken me?" I screeched at the sky.

Another arrow pierced me in the back. I screamed. Coughing blood, I crawled on twitching hands and knees to the top of the hill. My hands curled around something here, something that would save me, but my heart fell when the villagers surrounded me.

"You choose to martyr yourself then, girl?" The dark presence muttered. Yellow eyes, gigantic, frothing mouth, a ratty tail, waiting at the back of the mob, staring at me hungrily.

As I lay dying, a glimmer from the North Star caught my gaze. The villagers neared, their pitchforks and clubs hemming in the stars. A bright flash engulfed us all, and then pain everywhere, terrible pain…!

I gasped, hurling myself out of my blankets. For a moment I felt the lingering ache of arrow wounds. I clutched my ankle reflexively. The tree and smoldering campfire swam back into focus. A dream then.

I rocked back and forth. The red coals of the fire made the torches leap out at me again. Such a vivid dream. But it made no sense. Why would I have such a dream? Such brutish dreams. A foreign land. It felt like instinct, like memory.

Sleeping at night is unnatural.

"Look there. That must be Denver." I pointed to the town, etched in afternoon light. "We will be there by sundown."

Eithne shrugged noncommittally. Her stormy eyes were overcast, hiding her thoughts.

"In case anyone asks questions, you will be my sister."

"Why?"

"I cannot introduce you as a goddess, can I?"

"Oh. Very well."

"Do not do anything that will attract attention, please."

"What did you have in mind?"

"Almost everything you have done to date."

She crossed her arms. "So I have to be someone other than me."

I raised a quizzical eyebrow at her. "Is that a problem?"

"I am me. Why should I hide myself?"

"Because I am a priest, and you are a young woman."

She pondered that for a spell. "How do your women act, then?"

My suspicions confirmed, I looked to the sky beseechingly. I had been doing that enough lately to have developed pains in my neck. "Ladies are reserved, gentle, and discreet. They do not hang on men's arms. Nor do they shamelessly take advantage of a man's hospitality."

"Why did you offer, if I'm supposed to refuse?"

"The problem was not that you accepted it; it was the way you accepted it. If you carry on like you have, people might think…"

She blinked wide, interested eyes, and her ears perked. They actually wiggled. "Yes?"

"That you are a shameless woman."

"I am shameless."

"That is not what I mean." Once again, I was at a loss as to whether I should laugh or hide my face in embarrassment.

"I am a food goddess. I do not deal with human society except where your bellies are concerned. So speak plainly."

"Very well. They will think you are a whore."

She cocked her head. "What's a whore?"

My face sank into my hands. "Why me?"

Chapter 3

Late that afternoon, we walked into Denver. The dusty, bustling town was something of a letdown for me. I had been told that more people lived here than anywhere else on the Plains, but the population seemed pitifully small. Perhaps it seemed that way because I was used to New York.

The small number of people meant the lodgings were not the best, either. Nice enough, clean and tidy, but I still missed the luxuries of the cities in the east. It was, however, better than sleeping on the road. Since travelers had booked most of the lodgings, Eithne and I had to share a room.

Therefore, I was in a bad mood already, and desperately wanting a bath. I piqued Eithne's curiosity when I mentioned this in passing. "You wallow like pigs, then?"

"It is not a mud bath. How long has it been since you last took one?"

She shrugged. "It rains on me every once in awhile. I stopped paying attention to it."

"Does the smell bother you after a few hundred years?"

Eithne grinned wickedly. "That's the first joke you've attempted."

"It was not a joke, Miss Eithne," I said, straight-faced. "You are rather fragrant."

She pouted.

I left our room to take my bath. I had to haul the water up myself, so the sun had sunk below the mountains by the time I slipped into the rusty tub. The soap was grimy, but it sufficed. I avoided the brushes.

I eased out the aches from our long walk. Despite being either a liar or crazy, Eithne was more perceptive than I gave her credit for. One of my greatest ambitions as an adolescent had been to evangelize the Indians. Circumstances at home had hastened that ambition. That haste had left me with few funds. In effect, I was the one to blame for my current situation. I needed Eithne, and she said she needed me…for one reason or another.

Eithne. What a curious name. My grandfather had been an Irish immigrant. He had passed down some rudiments of old Gaelic, from when he was a scholar, to us grandchildren. Eithne meant something like grain, or seed.

The water cooled, and my hands began to pucker. If she knew Gaelic, that meant she might have learned it from the resurgence of the language fifteen or so years ago. Was she lying about her name? If she had lived out here all of her life, how could she know Gaelic? Why would she choose a Gaelic name? Perhaps she had heard a random word some stranger had spoken, and christened herself with it. But what did she gain from deceiving me in such a way?

Finally, I gave up my ruminations, toweled myself, and left to prepare for dinner.

The Cormac glanced at me out of the corner of his eye. I glanced back, fluttering my eyelashes.

"Please stop that," he growled. "I am supposed to be your brother, remember? Decorum."

"How can I when so many interesting happenings spring about us? They're like rabbits. I want to catch them all!"

He glared at me.

"Don't you like my eyes?"

He squirmed in his seat. I fluttered them again, just to annoy him. We were in the communal den, where everyone drank and ate. The fire crackled and chittered in the corner. It made me want to curl up and sleep. But the night was young, and that made me want to prowl.

Bored with my game, my gaze wandered until I spied two young humans kissing in a corner. Though the kiss lasted only an owl's blink, I found the transformation in the two fascinating. The young man smiled foolishly; the woman, shyly. As if she were privy to a secret happiness.

I looked at Alan up and down thoughtfully. "What is kissing?"

He had been startled by my question. He hid it well. Not fun at all. "What do you mean?"

"What purpose does it serve?"

His eyes flicked toward the couple in the corner. "There are many kinds of kissing. The French greet one another with a kiss on the cheek."

I pointed at the couple. "What about that kind?"

"Stop pointing." The Cormac leaned back in his chair. "That kind of kiss excites lust."

"Ah." I drew circles on the table with my nail. "What about other kinds?"

Alan was looking at me strangely. I wished he would stop. "Some," he finally said, "encourage love, rather than lust."

"What is it like?"

"Being in love?"

"No. Kissing."

"Eh…" The Cormac looked like a cornered chicken.

"Thet sounds like an invitation!" A grizzled man in a diseased sulfur-yellow hat injected himself into the middle of our conversation, spilling Alan's water. "Ope, sorreh."

Alan's feathers bushed. "I do not recall inviting you to our table."

He ignored the Cormac, plopping himself in a free chair while wiping up the water with a disgusting looking handkerchief. One of his eyes wobbled crazily in its socket, and his left forearm twisted about like a gnarled tree branch. "Thet sounded like an invitation, young 'un, kiss her already!"

I didn't know a priest's face could turn such a color. Alan glanced at me, then away. I smelled something more than embarrassment. "Who are you, old man?"

"Name's Brand. I've been waitin' fer a coupla pebble like you to show up."

His name sent squawks of alarm racing through my head, but before I could pinpoint why, Brand continued with, "If ye'r bound for the pointies this time o' year, it be madness." Brand scratched his stubbly chin.

"Pointies?"

"Mountain tops, lardbrain!"

"I must go there, regardless."

"Why yew wanna go up there? It be snowin' already!"

"To evangelize the Arapaho."

Brand's belly wobbled with his giggles. When his seizure subsided, he gasped, "Crazy man!" He sat back, and a sudden change came over him, as if he had switched brains. "So, yer crazy, too." The wobbling eye settled on me. My hackles rose. This man made my flesh creep. "I've been wantin' to go back in there."

"Why?"

"Gold, man! Gold!"

"I see."

"But I didn't want to do it alone. Dangerous, ya know. I know the mountains fairly well, figgered I could find someone headin' that way and help em out."

Alan looked at me again. The room chilled. I started to say, "He already has a—" but Alan interrupted me. "We'll take your kind offer."

What? Did he still not trust me? I wanted to hiss at him, but I settled for a venomous glance. Oaf. Chicken.

"So…yew gonna kiss her, or can I?"

I cringed at his pouty lips. I would rather bite off my own tongue. Alan gripped my hand, warning me to stay calm. Some of my anxiety drained away, as if he were siphoning it into himself. "We are siblings."

Brand's crazy eye rolled from me to him. He chewed on his fingertip lazily. "That be a bald-faced lie."

Alan blanched, but somehow managed to keep his face calm.

"What is a puppy preacher doin' with a young thing like this?"

"We are—"

"Don' lie to me, boy. I kin see through 'em like glass."

I felt like a chicken bone was lodged in my throat. Alan stared at Brand, and he stared back, like two wolves challenging each other. Brand shrugged. "If ye don' wanna tell me, thets fine. Was just…curious." He groaned, and levered himself out of the chair. "When yer ready to leave, meet me here. I'm always here." He left surprisingly swiftly for a man of his age and bulk. People leaned away from him as he went past. I sniffed. Yes, that was why.

I looked at Alan.

"He is only a man. If he tries anything, I can blast him off the mountainside."

"Can you now? I thought you were the goddess of corn."

I was about to shoot back a scathing retort, but the tinkle of broken glass sidetracked me. A drunken man reeled against the wall, staring blearily at a poster. "Hey, thas' funny," he slurred, pointing at Alan. "Yew look jis like…"

He toppled to the floor, snoring happily. All eyes in the room locked on us, an expectant, silent stare. A feverish chill crept into my knuckles. I smelled danger in the air, ripe cayenne-red, and the mustard stench of greed. Another lanky man ripped the poster off the wall. "Reward: Fifty dollars!"

Alan stood up, holding his hands out placatingly. "Now see here, gentlemen. This is all a misunderstanding—"

The whole room tipped toward us, sending every stinking human flying in our direction.

Fate seemed out to get me. For all my knowledge in the Word of God, I could not divert its path.

Every patron in the room hurled themselves at me in a messy avalanche. Before anyone laid hands on me, they started fighting among themselves over who would turn in the bounty. My hands felt like marble, frozen, as if to hold back the madness.

Eithne gripped my arm, and she led me through the whirlwind of bodies. One man stuck his leg out to trip her. She ground her heel into his knee. Another man leaped onto her back in a drunken frenzy. In an impressive, and unladylike, display of strength, Eithne dropped him to the floor, landing on him. She locked eyes with me. It could have been the light, but her gaze blazed red. "Run!" She screamed at me.

"I cannot leave you here!" I ducked a flying bottle. It shattered behind me.

"Yes you can!"

"But you are a lady!"

She swore like a sailor, pushing back a droopy-faced miner. Her nails seemed to bite through his shirt. I could have sworn I saw blood spots. She elbowed him viciously in the face, and he howled in agony, nose broken. "Do I look like one to you now?"

"But I am a man!"

"What does that have to do with anything?"

"I cannot leave you in danger!"

"I'm not in danger!"

She hissed in the face of a long-faced trapper. She knocked her fist into his temple and kicked him square in the gut, sending him staggering into me. He gripped my shoulders. I looked into his face, and rolled him to the ground. Eithne had knocked him senseless…or perhaps he had already been that way.

My wild companion gripped me by the shoulders, sticking her face into mine. The smell of her breath, a fragrant honey-chamomile, and of lupine, washed out the stink of the saloon. Curious, what the mind latches onto in times of stress. "I can't believe we're talking about this right now," she gasped.

"I would rather die than leave a lady in this pit of sin—"

A shotgun blast thundered through the room, freezing the writhing mob. Debris from the ceiling rained down on a noncombatant moodily sipping his beer. A voice equal to the shotgun boomed. "Shut up!"

All eyes, save for those dribbling on the floor, jittered to the barrel-chested officer of the law standing regally in the doorway. He glared around the room. The glare of his deputy swept in the opposite direction, to be sure they pinned everyone where they stood. "You all should be ashamed of yourselves, acting like this in front of women!"

"They started it!" a livid man bawled.

"Did they now?" The sheriff squinted at Eithne and me.

"They is wanted!"

"I am sure they are by somebody."

One patron, mostly intact, hobbled, picked up the dirty scrunched paper that had started the whole mess, and slapped it into the officer's hand. The lawman calmly gazed at the paper, then scrutinized me. "Well, he does look like him." He pointed the shotgun at me. "You are coming with us, boy."

I raised my hands imploringly, about to explain that this was all just a misunderstanding, when Eithne wedged herself between me and the lawman. I had never seen anyone so angry. Her lungs heaved like bellows, and her nails clawed at the air. She ground out her challenge from between her disturbingly long canines. "Come and take him then."

"Now, miss," the officer soothed, "I do not want any trouble here. Just come quietly and we can get this all settled."

I laid a hand on Eithne's shoulder. She whirled toward me, growling. I met her animal gaze. Her eyes glowed with a bloody fury…strange, horrible, heart-freezing.

"Listen to him, Eithne," I said, soothing the cornered wolf. Indeed, she bore a striking resemblance in the saloon's dim light. "Fighting will get us nowhere. Let us resolve this and be on our way."

For a moment, it looked like Eithne would ignore me and pounce. But then her ire drained. She shuddered as her strength deserted her, hunching into herself. "I don't like this, Cormac."

"I know. Trust me."

She hid her face behind her hair moodily.

"Now, I do not know what you did to get a price on your head, but the stocks are overflowing with scoundrels." The sheriff poked his shotgun into the small of Alan's back casually as he escorted us down the now pepper-dark street. Being a lady, they treated me with deference, although they eyed me like spooked hens. I winked at the sheriff's deputy. His face scrunched up, beet red. Somewhat satisfying, but not nearly as much as ripping his throat out with my teeth would be.

We stopped at a dark den with strangely shaped boxes in front. "Mortician's place," the sheriff grunted. "You will stay here while we question your lady friend."

"Sir, please let me explain first," the Cormac said, looking at me with horror. I rolled my eyes at him.

"Don't worry son, you will get your word in too. I am a fair man."

The sheriff poked Alan inside, shut and locked the door, then turned to me. "Come along, miss."

I squinted at him, then at the pitch-black behind him. "Do people normally creep behind arrested criminals?"

Our captor raised one eyebrow. "Sometimes."

"Who is that behind you?"

"Dad gum," the uninvited vulture muttered. "Lady sure does have sharp eyes."

The sheriff sighed and turned his shotgun into the dark street. "I would know that voice anywhere. Come on out, Larson."

A desperate looking youngling in a ragged shirt materialized from the darkness, holding a handgun. I nearly giggled at the names some Indian tribes had for those weapons. Then the Larson's hand shook as he pointed it at the door Alan had just gone through.

God had called me, but it seemed Satan had requisitioned me.

"Now, son," I heard the lawman's baritone rumble through the doorway. "Put the gun down before somebody gets hurt."

That sounded swell.

"You know I can't forgive him!" A young voice piped. An adolescent. "For what he done to pa!"

"Sheriff," Eithne's voice wafted through the planks, "This kit is not alone."

"Get the door open, then. I'll keep him talking."

"Would he shoot us?"

"Likely. He thinks he has nothing to lose."

So, the man I had been mistaken for was a murderer. Excellent.

"Boy," the sheriff said, "Don't—"

A shot ricocheted off the wall. The door rattled violently.

"Cormac!"

"What is it?"

"The door is stuck! Can you do anything from your side?"

"It's locked from your end."

"No, not any more."

Something slammed against the door. Eithne cursed. "Swearing will not help the situation."

"Shut up, Cormac!"

She slammed through it this time, plowing straight into me. I collapsed against an occupied coffin. The sheriff joined us, shooting as he backed into the mortuary.

"I feel like Ezekiel in the valley of dry bones," I muttered.

"Whazzat?" The lawman was still deafened by gunshot.

Eithne giggled.

"Miss, this is hardly the time for foolishness," The sheriff said, rubbing his ears. "We have to go out the back before they follow us in here." He pointed his shotgun at me. I took the suggestion and led the way to the back door. Before I had the chance to open it, a round shape burst through it, cackling as it did so.

"Come on, brothas!" he screamed, hurtling past us. "Brand's got some justise to dispense wi'!"

Brand threw himself at another man behind us. He dispatched him with his wobbling belly, slamming him into the ground and kicking him mercilessly.

"Go!" The sheriff waved his shotgun toward the door. Eithne took my hand, dragging me into the street. Brand followed us out, his cackle echoing off the surrounding buildings.

We stopped by a row of ramshackle sheds. "I think we lost them," the lawman panted. "We need to get back, find my deputy, get some guns and show Larson the gibbet." He pointed to me. "You say you are a preacher. You keeping with that?"

"I have no other story to offer."

"We need another gun." He handed me his revolver.

I promptly dropped it in the dirt. "I have never handled a firearm before."

He stared at the revolver. "I think I believe you, no matter what the wanted poster says."

"Johnson!" It was the deputy calling to us from a side street.

We scurried over to the deputy. Some barrels gave us a good hiding spot. From there we saw the entire opposite side of the main street, from whence another attack would likely come. I shivered. A gunfight was the last place someone like me should be.

Eithne scooped up the fallen revolver. She looked it over curiously, fingering the bits and pieces, sniffing the barrel.

"I will take that back, miss." Johnson held out his hand. "Did they see you?" he said to the deputy.

"No, we can take them by surprise—"

"I think I'll keep it." Eithne sighted down the barrel like a trained gunman.

"Have you shot one before?" The sheriff looked at her with one raised, bushy eyebrow.

"No," she said, and fired. Somewhere in the darkness, one of Larson's fellows gargled and fell heavily to the ground. Eithne winced. "Too loud."

"Good shot." Johnson peered over his shotgun into the gloomy street, waiting for more.

"I have an advantage. I can see in the dark." Eithne promptly fired again, grimacing at the crack and acrid smoke. Another ruffian sent his soul to God. "One to the left, near the bench," she growled.

Johnson's shotgun boomed, and a scream replied. Eithne loosed off another shot. "Missed!" Johnson scattered shot in the same direction. Eithne grinned morbidly. "Got him. Only two left."

"Take them alive," Johnson ordered. "Larson! Lay down your gun now."

"Never!"

The sheriff nodded at Eithne, who shot in the direction of the young man's voice. A startled yelp.

What happened next would remain with me for the rest of my life. Johnson and his deputy moved out of cover, their guns trained on the ruffians' hiding spots. Eithne jumped like a spooked deer and swung her gun arm about. The deputy threw himself in front of her. A shot. The deputy falling to the ground.

By now, a few enterprising, law-abiding individuals had reinforced us, picketing themselves in their houses and shop fronts. Lights were lit. Larson was in trouble and he knew it. He and his companion laid down their arms and faced us. Sheriff Johnson came out from behind the barrels. "Larson," he said, sighing. "What in hell were you thinking?"

"To right what been done to my pa…"

"This man did not kill your pa." Johnson looked around at the crowd, then back at the dead man walking. "I will thank you for one thing, and that is clearing up who this man is. He never held a gun in his life, son." He looked sadly to his deputy on the ground.

Larson shivered. His face fell. A sob escaped from trembling lips.

"Johnson, sir…"

"Padre. This man has broken the law and killed my deputy."

I took his meaning, and his glance. "I understand."

Eithne gripped my shoulder. "What will be done with him?"

She stared first at the dead man at her feet, then at the blubbering young man, innocently, with wide, curious eyes. It occurred to me that she might never have heard of a hanging before.

"To the rest of you all," Johnson pointed to the crowd. "Padre is off limits. He is not wanted."

"What will be done with him?" Eithne persisted. Her grip on my shoulder trembled. So she had been shaken.

"He will be hanged."

"What is that?"

Another officer was dispersing the crowd. Johnson took my hand and shook it. "Sorry for the trouble. I don't know what I can offer you for compensation."

I did. "A night or two's stay at the inn free of charge. I have come a long way, and used up most of my funds on my journey." It was a shame, but I needed what money I had.

"I will see what I can do." He slung his shotgun over one shoulder. "May I ask you to perform the Last Rites on my deputy, padre? He was Catholic."

So matter of fact. No tears clouded his face. I hesitated, but the sheriff continued.

 "You have to show up for the trial. Do you want to come to the hanging?"

"No, thank you." I turned back to Eithne, who still stared at Larson being led away by two volunteers. Back to the mortician's, I assumed. He dragged his feet, wailing incomprehensibly. I wished Eithne would avert her eyes. "It would not be proper of me to pray over him," I said to the sheriff. "Where does the local priest live?"

Eithne held my arm as we strode up the street to the priest's house. As we were about to step onto the pathway to the front door, Eithne stopped.

"Is something wrong?"

Her eyes were closed. She trembled, shook her head. "The men I shot."

"What about them?"

"They're dead." Something trickled out of her mouth.

"How do you—"

Eithne pitched forward, heaving violently. Liquid, black in the moonlight, splashed on the ground. "That's how I know," she gasped.

"Eithne!" I cast about, looking for someone on the street. "Someone! Help!"

I tried to pull away from her, to get help, but she held onto me with a clawlike grip. I gave in, and held her hair while she threw up.

"Oh, my." A new voice, crackling with age. "Come, I will help get her inside."

An old man—the priest—had come from the house. I had to take a second look at him. He looked extraordinarily like my father. Eithne staggered as we helped her to her feet. "It's fine," she said weakly. "I'm all right now."

"Do not be absurd, my child," the priest admonished. His sparse white hair whipped about in the breeze as he hefted Eithne's arm over his shoulder. She protested feebly all the way into the house.

We laid her on a hard bench beside the door. "I will get some water." The priest left.

"Are you truly well?"

Eithne gave me a look. "What do you think?"

"You did just cough up blood. I would not call that a good sign."

"If I say I'm well, that means I'm well!"

The priest returned. "Drink this." He handed Eithne a cup.

She screamed, knocking the cup from his hand. Startled, the priest stepped back. All of us froze.

I was the first to recover myself. "It has been a stressful night." I laid a hand on Eithne's shoulder. She twitched. Her breath came out in hard pants. She seemed to have realized she had crossed a line, for she said nothing, instead letting me talk.

"Father, we came here to…to tell you, that the deputy…Ah, I do not know his name. But…he is dead."

The priest straightened, his wrinkles drooping. "I see."

He took a coat off of his coat rack. "You are both welcome to stay and rest. Make yourselves comfortable."

Without further ado, he left. I sank into the first chair I saw. It was hard, solid. It felt good, after everything I had been through tonight. I felt the fear ebb from my body, to be replaced by annoyance, and an overwhelming desire to sink beneath bedsheets. "Eithne," I breathed. "Why?"

She ignored me. "Eithne."

"I know." She curled into a sitting position, hugging her knees. "I was discourteous."

"Very."

I noticed that she was shivering. She looked small. Her whole frame drooped. "Do you feel as horrible as you look?" I said.

Her forehead was resting against her knees. I sat beside her, bending to look at her face. Asleep.

She slumped sideways. I caught her head on my shoulder. I decided it would be best to let her sleep for now, so I let her stay there.

After some time, the priest came back. "We should carry her to the bed."

Eithne, in an uncharitable fit of pique, flopped like a sack of potatoes. We heaved and struggled together. She was much heavier than she looked. When that was finished, we went back out to his small dining room.

"Thank you," I said.

He waved my gratitude away. "It is no trouble. You have been through much. You are welcome to stay tonight."

"Thank you, Father…"

"Call me John, my child."

I nodded. "I wish to apologize for my companion. She can be…troublesome, at times."

He smiled. A wan smile, with little joy. "That troublesome nature of hers saved lives, I hear, one of them yours."

"Yes."

He nodded slowly. "It is a pity, though."

I was lost for words. He had lost one of his flock. I could not recompense him for that loss. No comfort I could offer would renew this fallen leaf.

"What is your name, my child?"

"Alan Cormac. I am a priest."

Father John frowned, his face crinkling. He shook his head. "That is what I heard," he said. Deliberately, as if wrestling with something.

Confused, I said, "Is something the matter?"

He met my eyes. "You are lying to me, my child."

Shocked, I averted my gaze. "What makes you think that?" I stammered. I had never been a good liar. And this priest reminded me too much of my father for me to lie.

He nodded. This priest must have had a gift of wisdom. He had seen right through me. "What are you trying to do with that girl?" He said sharply.

I only half heard what he said. "What?"

"Are you… taking advantage of her?"

"Of course not!" I exclaimed, flabbergasted. "I found her. Actually, she found me…"

He waved his hand again, and I fell silent. "Why are you pretending to be a priest?"

I shook my head. "I am…"

We stood there, facing each other. He, accusing. Me, shamed.

"Do you have a brush?"

It was Eithne. I saw the opportunity, and took it. "Come, Eithne. We cannot impinge on this man's hospitality any longer."

"But he said we could stay—"

I grabbed her hand, and whisked her out of the house, away from the quiet gaze of the man who looked so much like my father.

We went back to the inn, me, tired and bedraggled and in need of another bath, and Eithne becoming more and more chipper as we walked. Perky, like a spring sunrise. It was disgusting, how full of energy she could be after all of that. Perhaps letting her nap had been a mistake.

I opened the door to our two-bed apartment, sank onto my bed and closed my eyes. How to deal with her? With this whole catastrophe?

My mind refused to bring forth fruit. I drifted away into daydreams of a better life in New York. I could almost consider abandoning my quest. Almost, but not quite. I had invested too much in this endeavor. Turning back now would be defeat, surrender.

I strayed away from New York back to Eithne, who sat combing her hair on the other bed. It fell in red velvet strands about her shoulders, silky strands floating on a summer breeze.

As if she felt my eyes on her, she glanced in my direction. "You never answered my question."

"What question?"

"What is hanging?"

So, her curiosity would kill the cat, or rather the fox. Very well. She would find out how naïve she was. "You have honestly never heard of it?"

"I am often too occupied to pay attention to the odd habits of men."

"I see. Hanging is…" I searched for a delicate way to say it. "It is a form of execution."

"Execution?"

"A rope is tied about the condemned's neck, and then hung by it."

"So they are choked to death?"

"Not unless they are unlucky." My bile rose at the thought. My emotions were carrying me away. This conversation needed to end. "The procedure usually breaks the neck."

She shuddered. "How gruesome." She twirled her comb in her hands. Likely not her comb. Probably stolen. She seemed nervous, but her hair hid her face. "Are all humans so barbaric, then?"

"If you are who you say you are, you would know far better than me."

"I only speak to the people who tend the maize and squash, and rarely at that." She shook her head as if trying to get dust out of her hair. "Why is such a thing needed?"

"Discipline is required to live in a peaceful society. You protect the innocent by stopping criminals before they can do further harm."

"Do you hang all criminals, then?"

"Of course not. Most do not deserve hanging. We give them the chance to repent." Where once I would have said this with conviction, my voice suddenly seemed flat and gray.

"Why some and not others?"

"How do you mean?"

"Why do you hang some and not others?" she persisted. "Why do some get the chance to bury the hatchet?"

"All are given the chance to repent before God. I imagine Father John will go to Larson in the morning, if not now." I recalled her unbelief. My answer felt hollow. Flawed. I wondered if I believed it myself.

Eithne wiped her face, the back of her hand glistening in the flickering candlelight. "But he will still die." Her hand fell to her lap. "I don't like it."

I did something then that startled both of us. I laid my hand on hers. "I do not like it either. But it is necessary."

She had surprised me again. She had changed from a wild demon into a vulnerable girl…again. And, somehow, I could not think of her as a liar. Insane, perhaps, or even a victim of some strange plot, but not a liar. Not like me.

"Shouldn't I be hanged, then, according to your law?"

She had delivered the question in a pointed, matter-of-fact way. "Of course not," I answered. "You were defending yourself."

"How is that different? Was not Larson attempting to right a wrong?"

"You did not instigate it. You had every right to do so."

She touched her lips with a slender forefinger. "If only that were true," she whispered. "Why didn't you take the gun then?"

"I," I said indignantly, "am a priest. I have no experience with guns."

"Hmph." Eithne went back to combing her hair.

"Eithne…There is something I have been meaning to ask you."

"What is it?"

"Your name. Do you know what language it is in?"

"My language. The language I knew first."

"May I hear it?"

"Tá mé ceanúil ort." Eithne cocked her head. "Is that what you wanted?"

"I cannot make head nor tail of it. What does it mean?"

She winked. "It's a secret."

I sighed. "Play your games. I shall retire." I had thought we had been making some kind of progress, but instead she had descended into childish flippancy. I did not understand what went on inside her head. Perhaps, I did not want to.

I slept fitfully that night. I woke up frequently. Sometimes, I thought I heard a whimper coming from Eithne's direction as she slept, but then I drifted again, into memories of happier times.

The familiar-unfamiliar trees.

Flee!

The trees flying past me were unfamiliar, yet it seemed like they knew me.

Run!

The beating rabbit-thump of my heart.

Log!

I sprawled, cursing. The villagers, moments behind me. That terrible, cloying presence.

I scrambled to my feet, only to collapse again as my ankle betrayed me. The treeline picketed my path like iron bars. I clambered through the tangled wood and limped up the grassy hill. The stars glared down at me, so bright, as if eager to see them kill me.

An arrow zipped past me. I ducked, limped faster. "There's the girl!" Eerie red torchlight.

Another arrow. I collapsed, feeling the searing pain in my other leg! Sobbing, I clutched at handfuls of grass, pulling myself desperately up the hill. "Why have you forsaken me?" I screeched at the sky.

Another arrow pierced me in the back. I screamed. Coughing blood, I crawled on twitching hands and knees to the top of the hill. My hands curled around something here, something that would save me, but my heart fell when the villagers surrounded me.

"You choose to martyr yourself then?" The dark presence muttered. Yellow eyes, gigantic, frothing mouth, a ratty tail, waiting at the back of the mob, staring at me hungrily.

As I lay dying, a glimmer from the North Star caught my gaze. The villagers neared, their pitchforks and clubs hemming in the stars. A bright flash.

I woke. I bit my lip to keep from keening my terror to the night.

Chapter 4

It did not take long for the trial to arrive. Out here, the people of Denver carried out due process of law, and them alone. They took their duties seriously. Larson's trial ended in three days. Another two for the hanging. Eithne and I answered their questions to the best of our ability. Eithne went into great detail, though with less charm than usual. Throughout this time I scrupulously avoided Father John. For his part, he never mentioned my deception to anyone, for which I was both grateful and wary.

"I want to go."

"Why?"

"I want to see this."

"Some things are better left unseen."

"I want to go."

Warm morning light filtered through the window. Eithne chewed on her nightgown sleeve.

"Stop that," I said. "You will ruin it."

I took her sleeve out of her mouth. She growled. Then her gaze grew sly. She tossed her hair back and fiddled with the back of her nightgown. Preoccupied with forming an argument as to why she should not go, I did not immediately notice, and I barely turned around before the gown hit the floor.

"We are sharing a room out of necessity," I said, exasperated, "But you could do me the courtesy of warning me before you strip to Eve's clothing."

"I have to get ready if I'm going to go out," she said. I heard her rustling to find her clothing. "I don't really see the point of clothes." I could hear her smirk, and my face reddened. "Especially for women. They're so…confining."

"Indeed."

"You aren't going to convince me otherwise. I'm going."

I sighed. Perhaps it would be better to let her see this. It might rid her of her unbecoming spirited energy. I sighed. "Very well. But you cannot blame me for what happens."

I waited for her in the common area. She skipped down the stairs, radiant in green. Lively. I wondered if she truly understood what I had told her about the ceremony of death she was about to see.

She looped a hand into the crook of my arm. We walked together out of the saloon. The street was full of people, but those going to the hanging left a pall of silence in their wake. Eithne's hand was warm against my side. I focused on that hand, pretending I was walking in the park with Elizabeth, my childhood friend.

"Is something wrong?"

Eithne stared at me with owl's eyes, her head cocked. "Of course something is wrong." I blinked and looked away, surveying the streets. "I have never been to a hanging before. I will not relish the experience."

"Hmm." She chewed on her nail. I removed her hand from her mouth. She growled again. "Stop that."

"It is how I broke my little cousin's habit of sucking her thumb. If I am to teach you how to be a lady, I must resort to more drastic measures."

"I will bite you."

"Then I will thump you on the head." I sighed. "We have arrived."

The gibbet squatted in the square, the haglike crows cawing their prophecies of doom. I had heard stories of how bloodthirsty the Western settlers were—hangings were "a hog-killing time." Indian savagery morphed their faces into crippled parodies, like banshees, or wraiths reaching from the graves of vengeance. Not all looked on Larson with sympathy due his youth.

Eithne insisted on the front of the crowd; I, the back. In the end, we compromised.

They led Larson past us. Larson was as he had been the first time I saw him, and as I had seen him in court. Pale. Skinny. Frightened. Resigned. A woman with golden hair and white dress walked beside him. Eithne twitched, and whispered something. "Yes, I think it is his mother," I said absently.

Was it emotion or reason that told me he deserved his fate? Was it the hand of mercy or the fist of judgment which clenched my heart?

"Mother," Eithne whispered. Though the crowd seemed to take no notice of her, Eithne's eyes were locked on the woman.

"It is not polite to stare," I whispered. Eithne twitched in annoyance.

The crowd jeered. Larson stumbled step after trembling step to the noose. His mother must have been lost in the crowd. I had lost sight of her.

He stopped at the noose, which the executioner draped about his neck. The crowd stilled for his last words. He looked out at them, and I saw a glimmer of defiance. "It ain't right." Larson found me. His eyes were a sky blue, like Elizabeth's. "None of it. Hang the law."

As the executioner's hand grasped the trapdoor's mechanism, I caught a movement from the corner of my eye. "No!" My hand shot out, catching Eithne. "You fool!" I whispered hoarsely. "What are you doing?"

"Can't...Not!..." Eithne squirmed, but I restrained her, hugging her about the waist. A woman screamed. Noise swelled, the crowd building a crescendo. The noose tightened. The gibbet opened.

Larson hung suspended for a moment. This damned soul, a falling leaf, blown to the river Styx. In that moment, too, I saw the woman with the golden hair standing next to him, stoic, with the poise of authority and judgment.

I blinked. Larson's feet thrashed, then twitched feebly.

Eithne turned to me. I caught the hand she raised to strike me.

"How did you stop me?" I had expected tears. What I received was Eithne's blistering anger, her eyes wide, as if in fright.

"You could not have saved him." My throat felt constricted . I saw Brand across the crowd, grimacing, or smiling. "People are staring at us," I said. "Contain yourself. I beg of you."

Something –I doubt it was my words—had paralyzed her. I dragged her to the back of the dispersing crowd. She sat heavily on a wooden shop step. "Is this the law?" she whispered.

"Are you well?"

She shrank from my touch. "You think just like them."

My hand closed into a fist, which fell, impotent, to my side. "I warned you."

Her gaze flicked sideways, like a child caught tattling.

Brand sidled up to us. "So, now that's over with," he said cheerily, "when were you chilluns plannin' on makin' yer trip to the pointies?"

I studied Eithne. She stared at the ground, as if suddenly gone blind and deaf. "Tomorrow," I said. "It would be best for both of us if we left tomorrow."

The sun peeking over the horizon awoke me. In New York, I would never have risen this early, but the travails of the open road forced it upon me.

I dwelled on the meeting with Brand at…what time?…he had not said. He had said he was always here. So, I guessed it did not matter .

I slipped quietly out of the room, successfully avoiding waking Eithne. She had tossed and turned all night, waking me several times. I decided it would be best to let her sleep instead of taking her along. Though she would likely insist she could go without sleep, it would be best to give her some rest so I could avoid carrying her again.

I traipsed down the stairs with mixed feelings about the man who had offered his services, this Brand. He seemed to be a shady character, yet at the same time, I had no doubt he knew the mountains well. I had asked Sheriff Johnson about him, and he said he had gone into the Rockies before in search of gold. And he had helped us escape Larson. I had no rational reason to mistrust him.

But he had the same name as the trader who had dropped me off at Bent's Fort. It seemed…strange. If I had been inclined I would have chuckled. I sounded paranoid, like Eithne.

I reached the common room. No one was there. The morning had been given over to the souls of the dead.

My motives, which had seemed so clear before, had become muddled, murky. I was not sure what had confused them. Perhaps this doubt plagued all missionaries.

Eithne. The poor girl. Perhaps I should have been more persuasive. Then again, I could not convince her of anything. Once she set on something, she saw it through to the end. How could I combat her oak-brained notions and convince her I only wanted her good?

Her judgment of me. Comparing me to that rabble. I had wanted to physically remonstrate her, to flaw that perfect skin.

"Enjoyin' the scenery?"

Brand lumbered beside me. I choked on a squawk. "Ye…yes, I am."

His one good eye fixed on me while the other spun crazily in its socket. "Them pointies are beeooteeful."

"They are."

"But, they's dangerous. You hafta know what you doin'. Air's thinner up there, too. Ye need stamina."

"Do not worry about me. I have stamina."

"That ye do. But do ye have luck, too?"

"I do not need luck. God is on my side."

Brand chuckled. "I need to make some prep'rations. Yew should do likewise."

"I shall. After I take my fill of the mountains."

He nodded and waddled down the street, leaving me with my hopes, fears, and doubts. And a chill down my spine.

Curse you, Eithne. Curse your paranoia.

Sleeping at night. How unnatural. And how unforgiving.

My strange dream had left me restless, uneasy. I felt as if I had glimpsed something secret, hidden; like a stash of poisonous squirrel's nuts.

I sat up, untangling myself from my nest of blankets. Perhaps the dream had come from the bad feelings of yesterday, like eating rotten meat and the stomach then squirming. But the squirming didn't stop . If the dream was meant to purge, then it had failed. My feelings still roiled about me like trout leaping up the river.

I vowed never to sleep at night again, if I could help it.

I drifted down the stairs. Seeing Alan standing outside, I moved to join him, but just then, that disgusting Brand appeared like a badger out of its hole. I hid myself in the stairwell before he could see me and waited for him to move on.

Of course, I listened to their conversation. Brand seemed to be talking with two mouths. When he left Alan, I relaxed. Better.

I crept out into the communal den. Alan still stood there, staring at the cold morning. His shoulders slumped, as if a moose lay across them. He had Atlas' back. He may not have been good at thinking on his feet, but he was strong, firm. Even when he panicked, he could keep his senses, even if he sank his teeth into the wrong goals. He was a man. Not like any man I had met. But still a man. It was rather disappointing. That ripe blueberry fragrance had raised my hopes.

I blinked, and shook myself out of my daze. I padded up beside him, and looked at the mountains with him. "How are you this morning?"

"Why do you care?" he said bitterly.

"Did a badger bite you on the behind, or something?"

He chuckled reluctantly. But he said nothing.

"You're doubting yourself. I can see it. Right here." I touched between his eyebrows, where worry lines crisscrossed.

He took my wrist, and put it down firmly. "Please, Miss Eithne. Do not touch me."

"I won't if you tell me what's wrong."

"I am…thinking about home, is all."

"You wish to go home?"

"Not at all."

"Why is that?"

"It is a complicated affair."

"I have time. You can talk."

"I never wished to talk."

I glanced in the direction the disgusting man had left. "Have you had second thoughts about him?"

"No." He turned away from me.

"You should." I knew he was still listening. He couldn't act disinterested.

"He is perfectly respectable, even if he is a bit odd."

"He's dangerous."

"How?" Suddenly his face was in mine. "How, Eithne? Do you have any proof?"

I was tempted to hiss in his face, but thought better of it. I still felt...irritable, confused...after seeing that kit's neck broken. Being a human, he probably felt worse than me, not in his right mind, like a rabid wolf. So I forgave him this slight. "I have my instincts."

"Is that all you ever go on? Can you not provide me with some evidence?"

I had a feeling that he was asking two questions with one. "I see. So you still doubt me."

"A reasonable man would."

"What of your faith, then? How do you reconcile faith with this reason you speak so fondly of?"

He straightened his collar and his necklace. "Faith is nothing without reason."

"You could believe me. It would make things simpler." I toyed with a lock of my hair. "You are incredibly vexing."

"Indeed."

I raised my face to the morning breeze, sniffing the mountain air, the baking bread, the cold dust. Was this what it was like to wake up every day for a human?

Alan cleared his throat. "If…If you do not mind me asking…"

"Ask. I don't mind."

"May I see you? I mean…do you have proof that you are a goddess?"

I smiled. "Why didn't you ask before?"

"You—!" His outburst caused a passing woman to give him a feral look.

"Very well." I took his paw, our digits wrapping tightly. He tried to pull away.

"Only those touching us can see us."

He stopped squirming, though his paw still twitched. I closed my eyes and concentrated. I didn't use these powers lightly, but if it made him stop badgering me....

But, something was wrong. I felt nothing. I wasn't supposed to feel nothing. I should have felt the cayenne fire, heard the wildcall of wolves. But, when I called out, nothing called back. Only a cold, lonely void. I snatched myself back from it before it consumed me.

This had never happened before.

Apparently I had some effect on him, for he had fallen into a stupor. I released his paw. "The day is getting old. Go and get ready like that lumpy man told you to."

He came to his senses somewhat. "Yes...I must prepare..."

Alan wandered off like a goat in a daze. I rubbed the paw that had been holding his. It felt scorched. I smelled the faint smell of blueberries.

And there had been something else, as well. An unexpected thrill when I had locked my paw with his. A thrill of expectation, a wild hunting call from another place.

I tried to bury that feeling as I packed Alan's things. But the warmth lingered in that paw. An unsettling, unnerving presence, like an eagle's gaze, raised my ruff.

What was she?

I contemplated my hand. Something stirred in me that had been asleep, unknown, like a hibernating bear. When she had touched me, all of my doubts had been siphoned away. Now my rational thoughts floated on the surface of a calm, deep sea. Like oil and water. I had been ready to denounce her for her lies. But if she touched me, or even looked at me, those doubts faded away. I simply could not think her a liar.

Eithne was kind. Annoying, uncouth, loud, and disreputable, perhaps, but she was no demon. A demon would have looked fairer, and felt fouler. Eithne did not hide her faults; rather, she embraced them openly. Perhaps too much so. A quality beyond my capacity. Commendable, even admirable, in a way.

But if not a liar, or a witch, then what was she?

I had been walking in circles in front of the saloon. With a start, I remembered the preparations I had to make for the long journey. I looked around self-consciously and straightened my collar. In witch's company or not, I had to finish what I started. I had come too far to turn back now.

I went to the nearest general store and bought supplies. When I returned to the saloon, I avoided our room, and instead bought some cold stew from the night before. When the saloon keeper brought it out, I stared at it glumly. It was chicken stew.

I supped alone, attracting little notice from the growing traffic of patron in and out of the saloon. I did not want to talk to anyone.

Eithne chose not to come down until Brand met me again, for which I was grateful. She had packed all of my things for me into my travel-stained rucksack. I took it from her without comment, and she relinquished it with the same courtesy.

The three of us traveled west out of Denver, toward the mountains. Eithne said the Arapaho lived there. "I don't know how to get there from here, though." She sniffled and rubbed her nose as she padded quietly behind me. "I always flew there."

"I know a pass," Brand offered. "It ain't easy, but we kin make it to their territory in about four days if'n the weather don' turn sour."

"That does not sound too difficult."

"Hah!" Brand's belly jiggled. "Ye'r crazy and stupid. I told ye before, the air up there's thin. Man can't breathe proper. So he won't be able to run when the Arapaho come for his guts!"

"Are they truly that violent?"

"They kin be. I think yer safe with the girl, though."

I stifled my reaction. He grinned at me. Could he know? I glanced back at Eithne. She had been subdued the whole way, but now she studied Brand with narrowed eyes.

"Why?" I asked him.

"Well, warriors don' bring pretty girls with them."

"I suppose…"

We all fell silent again. We walked until the mountains swallowed the sun in their whitecapped teeth.

The snow and wind crusted us over. I don't like bitter mountain winters. I am a goddess of growing things and the plains. Long winters were counterproductive, useless. The land needed rest, but mountains were always comatose.

This was the second day of Alan's meaningless wandering since we had left the kit-killing town. The pass was wide, but the snow had reduced us to single file. It was unnatural snow. Too early for the season, even for the mountains. The creepy one was in front, making a big show of struggling, and Alan just ahead of me—truly bogged down and shivering.

The creepy one yelled something, but the wind snatched away his words. "What did you say?" Alan yelled back.

"Hold hands! Ye don' wanna get lost! I'll lead us to shelter!"

Alan took my paw. It was cold, but it warmed quickly in my grasp.

We slogged through that hideous snow for what seemed like many moons. At last we collapsed under a sheltered spot, not a cave, but a place out of the wind with almost no snow. Brand slumped against the rock face, wiping his face. "Why'd I agree to this agin?"

"You offered." Alan panted. He still hadn't let go of my paw.

"Padre, yer crazy te try this."

Alan grunted. He looked at me. "How are you still so warm?"

I blinked. "How do you chill so quickly?"

Alan dropped my paw. The piercing cold immediately wrapped me in shivering sheets. I was not equipped to deal with this kind of cold yet. It made me want to sleep. I wanted to bury my face in his side just to be rid of the cold.

Thwump.

The sound perked my ears. "Did you hear that?"

"Hear what?"

I pressed my finger to my lips. "Listen."

Thwump.

I tackled Alan, forcing us both back onto the pass. "What are you—!"

"Rockslide!"

Rocks crashed down the mountain in a flood. Alan's eyes widened, but I was already dragging him down the pass. I slammed my shoulder into his, and we fell under an overhang.

A boulder the size of a buffalo sailed over us, showering us with pebbles. Alan threw himself over me. "Gerroff!" I tried to say, but he rolled us closer to the cliff face, so I had no opportunity to scold him.

At last, the crashing and thumping stopped. "Are you all right?" Alan said.

"Swell. This happens every day." The rocks had pelted us both, but we were on the edge of it, so it did us no real harm. "You look worse than me."

We staggered to our feet. "What of Brand?" Alan paused in the act of brushing himself off, staring at the top of my head. "What are those—"

"Don't thank me yet." I had heard something else over the rockslide. Something terrifyingly familiar. My ears twitched. My heart lurched. "I don't...It can't be!"

"What is it?"

Further up the pass, the rocks had clumped together like deer droppings. Yellow eyes crested the top of the pile. A huge muzzle, paws that could squish badgers, and a ratty tail, crusted with teething frost. My nightmare stood before me. The dark animal from my dreams.

Alan's back was to it, but he saw my face. He turned toward the monstrosity. "Dear God in Heaven! Is that a Fenris wolf—"

The coyote howled. I screamed, clutched my head. I wanted to make it go away, anything to make it go away! "Help," I whimpered.

Alan grabbed my forearm and dragged me down the pass. The coyote bounded after us, its feet kicking up plumes of snow. Nearer, nearer! Those bloodthirsty eyes! "No—!"

It collided with Alan, sending him spinning through the snow. The coyote stood over me, slavering jaws, quivering nose, bloodshot yellow eyes.

A strange feeling awoke inside me. It thawed my terror. I felt my power draw into me. With trembling hands, I shoved the coyote in the chest!

It fell back, winded. I staggered to my feet. The blazing red fire obscured my vision. Yes, I would change into my true form. I could defeat this coyote then. It was a stick, its ribs almost puncturing the taut skin.

"What is this?" Alan whispered. Through the howling wind, I heard the whisper. My ears twitched, swiveled to hear him. My tail swished in the wind.

I focused myself inward. I drew on the power, until it became a vortex within me. The fire enveloping me melted the snow.

I could feel Alan's stare of disbelief. "How is this possible?"

The shouts became whispers. That faint smell of blueberries…

The coyote snarled, and came at me again. I braced myself for the impact. It tackled me, throwing me back into the snow, and barreled straight for Alan. It swatted him brutally to the ground, snapped him up in its jaws by his coat. He struggled feebly, blood dripping down his forehead.

"Please don't," I pleaded. "Don't hurt him."

It met my eyes. Malevolent intelligence. Hatred, and cunning. It pawed the snow. Alan dangled limply, too weak to resist being dragged through the snowdrifts.

It stopped three wheat-lengths from me. Alan still dangling from its jaws, it growled.

"What is this man to you?" the coyote said.

"I…"

"Give me your power, and I will let him live."

"My power?"

It snarled. "Give it to me!"

"I don't know! I can't—"

It roared. The sound echoed off the mountains. I sank to my knees. "I can't!"

"Then he dies!"

I stretched out my hand. Could I stop it with such a puny limb?

It trotted to the edge. The Coyote met my eyes once more. A challenge. Its authority, its dominance, radiated from those hungry yellow eyes. Ravening strength coursed from those hungry limbs, and the teeth bit like the blizzard.

With a great sweep of its head, it threw him over the edge, down with the rest of the rockslide. I shrieked. Before the coyote could pounce on me, I stumbled to my feet. I threw myself after him, into the wild wind and swirling snow.

I awoke face-down in a snowdrift. The blizzard had coated me with a fine dusty layer, stained red with blood from my lips.

I groaned. Where had Alan gone?

I could barely move. I had never been so cold, felt so helpless. How could a goddess feel helpless? I pawed at the snow, and finally managed to lift myself to take in my surroundings. Alan lay not far from me.

My heart quailed. I crawled over to him, laid a hand on his cheek. So cold! "Alan, wake up!"

He laid still as a possum. I pressed both hands to his cheeks, laid my forehead against his, and screamed. It echoed off the mountainside.

He groaned. My breath caught. Still alive! "Alan, I—"

He mumbled something.

"What?"

"Cave. Dig…snowcave."

"Wh—Why?"

"Wind… warm. Freeze to death."

I pawed frantically at the side of a snowdrift.

"Parallel to… wind."

I obeyed his instructions. I needed them. I could barely remember the most basic movements. Time was lost to me as I scooped pawful after pawful.

Alan would freeze before I finished. I looked at my paws. They were raw from scraping the rocks when I had fallen down here.

I saw the sudden flash of the snow melting around me when I had faced off with the coyote. I called on the power again. It was weak…or maybe I was weak. But the fire leaped into my paws, and the snow melted away before it. Alan stared at them. "What…"

"Hush."

Soon I had a small snow cave dug out of the whitetooth snow. When I crawled back to Alan, he had closed his eyes again. I took an arm and attempted to drag him, but he was too heavy. I wanted to sob, and I despised myself for it. All of this, to be defeated now? Where was my strength when I needed it?

I slapped him. He twitched. He was conscious enough to help me move him. "Dratted pack," I muttered. "You weigh as much as a buffalo." I stuffed him through the hole first, then shuffled in. It was dark, but already it felt warmer.

I laid Alan's bedroll between us and the snow, and curled around him. My cheek rested against his. With the dregs of my power, I warmed myself, heating his shivering limbs. I could not die from cold. Nature cradled me. But nature did not coddle men. I mediated between him and nature to save his life, taking the warmth from the life of the slumbering trees. They would renew the air in our little cave as well.

His breathing steadied. His trembling fingers quieted when I locked my hands in his. My eyes felt itchy, and my limbs felt like dead tree branches. I fell asleep.

Chapter 5

"So you choose to martyr yourself?"

I shivered. The trees closed in around me, those menacing shapes of the villagers poking at me with their pitchforks.

"What is he to you?"

Vile. Violent.

A boy —just a kit— dangling from a rope.

Unjust. Destructive.

"What is he to you?"

I sat bolt upright, hitting my head against the ceiling of my makeshift cave. Dim light penetrated from the entrance. Back in the real world again. The nightmares already fading.

Our clothes had become wet. I picked at mine distastefully, then lifted the hem of my shirt. Alan's hand grasped my wrist. "What are you doing?"

So he was awake. "Taking off my shirt. It's wet. I want a new one. Fortunately I had the presence of mind to drag our things in here."

He stared at me. "I suppose that would be a good idea."

Surprised, I eyed him. "Are you feeling well?"

"You should ask yourself that first."

It was true. I had started shivering again. I cursed in the tongue of the native people. This shivering was annoying, and for some reason I couldn't stop it.

"You change first. I will look away."

He turned over. I peeled off my wet clothing and put on the dry change Alan had bought me in Denver. I slithered and twisted to get them on correctly in the cramped snow den. When I had finished, he sat up. He began to lift up his shirt, but stopped. "Are you going to look away?"

"Oh. Yes."

I heard his shirt slide wetly across his skin. Unable to resist completely, I peered out of the corner of my eye. He truly had a beautiful back. I wanted to touch it, but I knew he wouldn't approve. But…that hadn't stopped me before, had it? I had taken what I needed from him before. I had always taken what I needed. Now it seemed…strange. Wrong, like a breach of some unspoken agreement. To touch him would change something.

So I didn't. I contented myself with looking.

I crawled out of the den first. The sun had just peeked over the mountains, the whole world covered in heavy white. We had tumbled about thirty wheat-lengths down the hill over rocks and boulders. A miracle that Alan had survived at all. Old pinewood trees, leaned over us in a tangled, hairy mess.

I had dug our snow den into the side of the mountain. The pass above us seemed miles away, out of reach. It would take many hours to reach where we had started, and neither of us could scurry like rabbits. I had been utterly exhausted. A bone-deep ache, as if I had aged a hundred years. Draining, like a creek without a source.

I held up my hands. They trembled. Lines I had never noticed etched my skin in stark relief. The whole world was icy. Nothing grew. Everything in stasis, waiting for spring. It was a time to sleep, not to climb mountain passes, or confront my waking nightmares.

Alan hauled himself out of the snow den, bringing our things with him. He limped to my side, breathing heavily in the thin air. "What do we do now?"

I raised an eyebrow. He had been the one with all of the plans, not me. "That's your decision. You either continue on, or you go back."

A stubborn line etched itself across his forehead. "I cannot go back. I have traveled too far to turn back now."

"Very well." I took a deep breath. "I…"

What would I say? I didn't know how he would react. Maybe I should just say it. "I'm ha…"

"Yes?"

"I…know where we can find the Arapaho."

"That is not what you were going to say before."

Sometimes he was incredibly dense, and sometimes he was far more perceptive than I liked. Telling him I was having troubles with my power would give him all sorts of fuel for his fire. I did not want to listen to another lecture on his god.

"It is fortunate that you know where the Arapaho are," he continued. "I do not think we will ever find Brand again." He looked up the mountain. "I hope he is alive."

"That old man is indestructible."

"I am not sure that translates to surviving a rockslide."

"He had been blessed by the gods."

He glanced at me sideways. "Is that why you do not like him?"

"I do not care whom the gods choose to bless. I care which gods choose to bestow their blessing. And that man was blessed by a trickster."

He was struggling with something again. "What did I see?"

I cocked my head. "What are you talking about?"

He avoided my eyes. Sweat beaded on his forehead. "What are you?"

I wanted to claw his eyes out. "You still insist on unbelief, even when I have said, time and again—"

"Either you are lying to me, or..."

"Or what?" I poked him in the chest. "Have I ever lied to you?"

He gritted his teeth. "I do not think now is the best time for this conversation." He began to pick over his belongings, ensuring everything was still there. "We need to move if we are to make the best use of daylight."

He took a few steps, then collapsed into the snow. I rushed to his side. "What hurts?"

He rolled over, grimacing. "My knee."

"You fool." I cursed. "You stubborn fool."

"Help me up."

I did as I was told. He grimaced as I lifted him up easily. "As long as you hold me up, I can walk." He looked up the mountain, eyes squinting in the gathering light. "Now to the Arapaho."

He still would not give up. Everything conspired against him, and he hit his head against his fate like a moose. "I don't know how much help the Arapaho will be willing to give," I said.

"I refuse to go back." He was panting, his eyes glazing over like cold lard on bacon. I wished for some bacon wistfully.

"We would still have another two days of travel, even if you hadn't been injured." I began to walk forward, supporting him gingerly. I didn't know where to put my hands, how to hold his weight. I had never carried the burden of human life in this way. Only my god-strength kept me from dropping him.

We crawled up the mountain, up the pass, until we reached the rockfall once more. Sometime in between, Alan fell asleep. I fumed all the way up. I, who flew with the birds, who whispered to the corn, was forced to trundle up a mountainside like an earthbound animal. I was making better time than we had been before he had been hurt, ironically, because I could jog with him on my shoulder. Why did I bother with such a weakling?

Why…why did I bother? It set off a wellspring of emotions inside me. It stirred them like the breeze stirred the trees, set the restless leaves twirling, wriggling out of my grasp like rabbits. The only thing that I was sure of was the promise I had made to him, to help him with his goal. I had made that promise out of curiosity, but I never broke my word. Though, I hadn't foreseen this predicament…Perhaps Mother was right. She always said I was too curious for my own good.

The sun was out now, but the nighttime cold still clung bitterly to the small breeze. The mountain pass was easy enough to traverse, but we still had a long way to go before we could find help from the Arapaho. I had not visited them in a very long time—long even for me. They were hunters of buffalo, not growers of corn, squash or beans.

I did not normally worry this much. But so many things had become strange to me. I could no longer rely on my own power. I shuddered as I remembered it, the cold, lonely emptiness in which I had groped, expecting the flooding warmth. What was I without it?

The coyote had demanded I give it my power. I didn't know what that meant. Gods had never exchanged powers before…had they? Stolen artifacts, or subdued each other, maybe. How could another god hear the whispers I heard? Where would they receive the knowledge to understand them?

This coyote was a consumer. Its howl had been of unbearable, solitary hunger. The howl had been the howl of that void, of abandonment.

I stumbled. The valley stretched out before me, a wide canvas, the jagged teeth of the mountains ready to swallow the sun. I had walked several hours without stopping. Alan fell from my shoulder into the snow. He seemed very drowsy, but I needed him awake to tell me what to do. "Sorry," I said. "You can't sleep now."

I laid my hand on his forehead. I breathed in and out slowly, preparing my power.

"Are you a spirit?"

The question came from a young voice, in a tongue I knew well. I turned to see a young hunter. He was Arapaho. He clad himself in deerskin. A rifle dangled loosely about his shoulders. I guessed him to be about twenty years, probably less. I wasn't good at determining ages. He could have been fourteen and I wouldn't have been able to guess. Humans were unpredictable that way.

"Your tribe is late leaving the mountains this year."

"Yes. Fall came later than it has before, and the buffalo migrated later. We will be moving soon." He pointed to Alan. "What is this white man doing with you?"

"He is in need of my help. His knee is unbalanced."

"Come with me."

He knelt beside Alan. Looking at his exhausted face and battered limbs, he clucked disapprovingly. "Quickly. We must get him to the teepees."

We trudged for another hour. Alan kept nodding off, but the Arapaho would nudge his head whenever he was in danger of going to sleep. He kept looking at him sideways, in a way I didn't like, but he was helping us. I helped when I could, but I had reached the limitations of my human form. My feet hurt unbearably. My eyes drooped.

We made it to the village. It was nestled within some pines next to a small, rock-cold creek, which bordered a large frosted meadow.

The people came out to greet us. Men and women of all ages, all sizes, the tribe was large and prosperous. Two older men separated themselves from the rest. The smaller more crooked one held a bowl, from which the scent and smoke of sage wafted into the air. He stepped between us, then bowed in the four directions, north, east, south, and west. He said in a ceremonial chant, "We welcome the spirit who has chosen to visit us on this day."

I chafed, irritated. He stepped back, and the other man stepped forward. "Welcome, spirit. We have prepared for you with all the proper ceremonies, for we received your message four days ago in a dream."

This man had the bearing and demeanor of an alpha male. He had a strong, wise face. Everyone gave deference to him unconsciously. "Please see to this man," I said. "He was injured during his travel here." The chief nodded and motioned another man to relieve me of my burden. They bore him away into one of the teepees. I swayed, my legs threatening to fold. My vision flickered.

A large white aura appeared beyond the village in the meadow. A great white buffalo stared back at me. It tossed its head to the mountains in the west.

I blinked, and the buffalo vanished. In its place was the face of the chief. "What is your name?" I asked him.

"I am Chief Left-Hand. Do you require anything more from us?"

"A place to rest." An Arapaho woman led me to a teepee. I sank into the soft hide bed, and the world slipped away from me.

I awoke late the next evening. My head felt stuffed with burrs. The headache had come on because I had slept at night. Dratted Alan, making me sleep at night.

I rose out of the blankets. They were warm and comfortable, and I didn't want to leave them, but the Arapaho were making too much noise. How had Alan fared?

I crawled out of the teepee, narrowly avoiding burning myself on the smoldering bowl on the ground. The medicine man had been smudging again. An annoying practice, but at the same time, calming.

I breathed in the smoke from the burning sage. The teepees were decorated beautifully with images of the tribe's history. Men and women went about their bug-ant work. They seemed not to notice me, as if gods and goddesses strolled through their midst regularly. Perhaps they did.

I was not very familiar with the Arapaho. I could speak their language, but beyond that, I had little knowledge of their customs.

The young one who had helped me carry Alan came before me, offering me food from one of two bowls. "Did you sleep well?"

"I did." I took the bowl and began eating. It was pemmican; dried meat ground and formed into bars. "What is your name, boy?"

He sat to my left, enjoying his meal. "Kuruk."

"Bear. A good name."

He puffed out his chest. I chuckled, but on the inside, so I would not embarrass him. "My dream said I was to help you. If you need anything, I will be glad to give it."

I looked out onto the meadow covered with frost. "So it was you who had dreamed of my coming."

"Are the white men going to go away? Are they surrendering?"

"I do not know."

"But you brought a white man here." He flexed his bull-arm.

"I cannot speak for the white men." I eyed his arm appraisingly. "But I am sure, any white man would flee from such a great warrior as you."

The battle fire lit in his eyes. I smiled, amused. "Tell me, Kuruk, what does the buffalo mean to your people?"

The battle-fire turned to confusion. "Do you not know the buffalo spirits?"

"I know the foxes. I know the rabbits. I know the corn, the beans, and the squash. All I know of the buffalo is that they trample my crops."

He seemed to accept my explanation. "The buffalo are wise animals. They give us their wisdom and guide us to the next hunt. But there are much fewer now. Chief Left-Hand says it is because the white men have slaughtered many of them. They attack our Cheyenne brothers with no declaration of war." His face hardened. "The white men will pay for that."

I was about to admonish him, for the people of this land had not always been kind to the buffalo either. "Enough, Kuruk." It was Chief Left-Hand. "Do not let your heart become clouded with thoughts of vengeance. The white men in the Boulder Valley have been peaceful."

Kuruk, put out, pouted. I found it charming, if a bit irritating. Then again, almost everything had been irritating me recently.

"Kuruk, go do something useful." Left-Hand waved him away, smiling. Kuruk grumped and stomped away to sulk. "Your gaze stretches into the meadow," Chief Left-Hand said, sitting next to me. "What do you see?"

"I see a white buffalo."

The Chief grew still, like a hunter about to pounce. "You are certain of this?"

"I think it wants me to follow it."

Chief Left-Hand peered at me curiously. He seemed almost taken aback, as if I had said something…not rude, but…unexpected. Perhaps, sacrilegious, if such a word could be applied to these people. I had learned that crunchy word from Alan. "So, you have not come to give us direction?"

"I'm sorry, Chief Left-Hand, I have not. I was guiding that white man to your people. He had a message for you."

"Is it about the buffalo? Will the white men stop slaughtering them?"

"No, it wasn't about that."

His shoulders sagged. Then he straightened. "It is good that you have seen the white buffalo. It is a sign that this winter will be more prosperous. Still, our fate is uncertain with the whites roaming the land at will. They will not honor the agreements they made with us twelve seasons ago. That has angered some of the more battle-hungry warriors. The Dog Soldiers continue to hunt on the lands we gave to them. The white men do not like that. Some are peaceful, but…" He squared his shoulders. "If they wish for a battle, then battle we shall give, along with our Cheyenne brothers." He shook his head. "I am sure you do not want to listen to all of this. You are not an ancestor, or a spirit who watches over us."

"I watch over all of the people in this land, even if they don't grow corn."

He seemed to ponder that for a moment. He asked, "What is your name?"

"Eithne."

"Do spirits have vision quests? I thought that only the living could have such quests, for they come from the spirits."

A vision quest was something all people of this land did when they sought guidance. They would wander out in the woods for days, or they would sit in a hut with hot rocks and steam themselves, until a vision came to them. "I don't know, Left-Hand. I am not on a vision quest."

"But you are seeking guidance. Otherwise, the White Buffalo would not have appeared to you." He stood up, clapping his strong hands. "Let me consult with the medicine man about this. He may know what we must do."

The Arapaho, like all of the natives of this land, wasted nothing, especially time. Chief Left-Hand strode back into the forest of tents. I was left to brood. For once, I had nothing to do. It was…strange. I had tried to avoid this moment, this stillness. I didn't like it. I wanted to move.

Following this compulsion, I stood, and sprinted into the field. I would follow the white buffalo.

I met her in the forest, in the deep shadows of the pines. She was a great white beast, with deep-set dark eyes. All the world around her brightened, as if her knowledge illuminated everything. "Eithne," she grunted. "It has been a long time."

"Do I know you?" My memories stirred, but I never dealt with the spirits of the buffalo, not unless they trampled my crops.

"Perhaps you know this form better." Suddenly, the buffalo vanished in a breath of white light. In its place a tall, blonde woman stood, clad in white cloth, rooted as a sequoia. An owl alighted on her shoulder. A branch of exotic fruit was tucked beneath her arm.

I smiled and bowed my head. "Mother," I breathed. "It is good to see you."

"And you, youngest." I detected her pleasure in seeing me, but also the stir of silent snowfall, the sigh of falling leaves.

"Have I disappointed you? Did I fail in some way?"

"No, my dear. I am wondering what it is you have brought here."

She gazed past me, back toward the village. "I'm not sure what to make of him, myself. He is different from other priests."

"Many of his religion have come across these lands."

Surprised, I stared, my head tilting.

"Really, Eithne. You haven't been paying attention to the past four hundred years?"

"I deal in plants. They are slow to notice change."

"But you are also the guardian of the fox."

I hung my head. "You are the one who deals in religion."

"It is not important now, my dear. What is important is what this man might represent."

"What is he, then? Do you know what god has blessed him with this power?"

Mother's owl hooted. "We will speak of him later. Coyote has found you."

A cold bolt of fear raced up my spine. "How? When will he be here?"

"You do not have long."

I took a breath. I wasn't sure how Mother would react to this news. "There is something you should know."

"Yes?"

"I promised to be by his side. At first it was just out of curiosity. But I can't break my word to him. Please, can you do anything?"

She seemed to take it well, but I had never been good at reading her signs. "I cannot, not if Coyote has good reason to hunt him. But if you want to protect him, you must leave. Has he ever lied to you?"

"No, he hasn't." I breathed deeply. "For how long must I leave?"

"As long as it takes. You may never see him again."

I closed my eyes. The weeks I had spent with Alan had been...I wouldn't have called them pleasant. So, why did the eye-rain cloud my sight?

I searched my heart, found that which Alan had planted inside me, and tore it out, as a weed to my three sisters.

I met Mother's gaze once more. "Do I have time to say goodbye?"

"If you hurry."

The Arapaho village had gone to sleep. I padded in, and found the tent where Alan rested. I stirred the front flap to see if he was awake. I crawled inside, my paws padding on soft leather.

He looked so peaceful. His brow, normally furrowed, had smoothed. His posture, once uptight and rigid, became careless in sleep.

I stared at him for awhile. Then, aware of my limited time, I came to a decision. With trembling fingers, I took his head in my hands, and kissed him on the forehead. I gave him my blessing. I had devoted a certain amount of my power to him forever, lost to me forever.

"Alan. I suppose this is the end."

Mother whispered to me from beyond the trees. "The Coyote approaches."

I took a deep breath, and left the tent. I wandered beyond the village. I wanted to look back, but I knew that would be a mistake. I left him, the solitary fox, to wander among her beloved ears of corn.

My thoughts whirled around in a muddy pool. I found myself back in New York, at my family's table, shaking hands with my cousin. This dinner had been for his departure. It had been joyous, but also melancholy. We did not know how long it would be before we would see him again. "Send me a letter when you get to Denver," I said.

"I will," he promised.

As the dinner ended, he drew me into a private room. Red drapes hung from the windows, and elegant armchairs surrounded tea-tables. "When I send that letter," he whispered, "Will you be ready?"

I looked out the partially closed doorway. "I think so."

"Good," my cousin growled.

I turned back. Its teeth buried in my cousin's arm, there crouched a huge, yellow-eyed, hungry coyote.

My eyes snapped open. My heart raced. Just a nightmare, then. A nightmare, mixed with memory.

 I was in a large hide tent. Leathery skins wrapped me in a warm cocoon on the bare earth. Brand must have dragged me here. We had finally arrived in the village of the savages.

I scratched my head. That was not correct. What had happened? My dream kept getting in the way of my recollections. The coyote, still fresh from the nightmare, bled into my memories. Had I faced a giant coyote?

I almost laughed. Then the memory of the snow cave came back to me. She had dug it. She had faced that monster, rescued me from freezing to death, and dragged me here. She had, not Brand.

I owed her for that.

I tried to get up, but my right knee would not bend. It throbbed horribly. I felt along it, and realized someone had tied a splint to it. I buried my face in my hand.

A woman crawled in. She was clad in deerskin, and she held a bowl of dried meat in her hands. "Where is Eithne?" I asked her.

She gestured with the bowl. I took it. Of course, she would not understand. I would just have to wait, then. Eithne had promised to be my translator.

The woman went back outside. I finished my meal. Just as I was beginning to drift back to sleep, another person crawled into the tent. It was a man, middle-aged, with eagle feathers stuck into his hair. He extended his hand to me.

"I am Chief Niwot," he said. "Left-Hand."

"My name is Alan Cormac," I replied politely, surprised that he spoke English. "That girl who was with me. Do you know where she is? I want to speak with her."

"She is gone." He waved his hand south.

"Could you send for her?"

"I cannot. She has told us to take care of you."

He did not seem overly pleased. I would be a burden, another mouth to feed. Therein lay my opportunity, perhaps. If I could prove myself useful to them, I could earn their trust. I could ask for Eithne's help, as well. I needed to learn everything I could about these people. "I have some skill with a needle," I said helpfully. "And some experience hunting deer."

"You will not hunt with that leg."

"I can cook. I can gut the deer for you."

He grunted. "You are here because the spirits sent you. She said you had a message."

"It is a message for all of your people…" I trailed off. How could I tell them now?

He grunted again noncommittally.

"Do you know when Eithne will be back?"

"I told you. She is gone."

"She…where did she go?"

"I do not know. She did not tell me."

I lay back among the blankets. So, she had finally left me, then. I had ceased to be of interest to her. She had led me here, and then abandoned me. I was finally free of her troublesome plots. How could this freedom feel so much like betrayal?

Now that I was here, I did not know where to begin to teach these people about salvation. I was no longer sure of it myself. The gods had made themselves known. The solid earth of reason had been eroded by the wolfish bite of the lupine's roots.

"You are younger than I expected, white man."

I sighed. My breath rattled like the autumn leaves. "I do not feel young. Not anymore."

Chief Niwot left the tent, and another man came in bearing something hot to drink. It made me drowsy, and I fell asleep once more.

Chapter 6

Most of the tents –teepees—had been taken down, strewn about like huge corpses as the Arapaho packed them.

I took the cloth of a smaller one and dragged it toward a horse, struggling with its weight. The medicine man had wrapped my knee firmly with cloth and sticks to keep it from bending. Kuruk finally came over and helped me the rest of the way. He hefted it onto the horse, then looked me up and down.

He never said anything, not in English, but I could see it in his eyes, the contempt. Chief Niwot had told me about his dream, but if such things were to be believed, then helping me obviously did not mean liking me. Why he held me in such contempt was beyond me. I had not done anything to him, and I was helping as best I could.

The medicine man clucked as he watched my antics. He tapped my injured knee, and I fell to the ground, writhing. "What was that for?" I gasped.

"He says he cannot heal it," Chief Niwot said. He had been passing by with various odds and ends, tucking them into packs on the horse's backs.

I felt a pang of worry at his words. "I'm sure it will heal eventually…"

Seeing my expression, the medicine man shook his head, muttering to Chief Niwot. "No, holy man. It will not. It was a wound a spirit inflicted." He leaned in as the medicine man muttered some more. The chief nodded, and stroked his chin. "He would have had you visit the healing springs, but that is too far to walk on your leg, and we are going down the mountain. He says there is one way it can be cured."

"Tell me, please."

He seemed to chew on the thought for awhile. He finally said, "Look over there, on the top of that mountain. There is a rock that looks like a thumb. Can you see it?" He pointed. "It is called Devil's Thumb. Once the Ute and Arapaho fought over this land. There we buried the devil, but left his thumb out to remind us of the evils of war."

"How will that help me?"

"I do not know. Neither does he." Chief Niwot put an arm around the medicine man. "He said he had a dream last night. If you make it to the top of that mountain, you will be healed." He turned his back on me. "We will be leaving soon. I will give you food enough for four days. That will be enough for you to make it there and back. It is your choice. We will be in the Boulder Valley." He turned to me again, his savage face unreadable. "The fox spirit said you had a message for us. Will you give it now?"

"It would take a long time to explain." I felt a surge of hopelessness at being left to my own devices once more.

Forced to take the steps of faith when I had neither capacity nor desire. Even my god had abandoned me.

Chief Niwot patted me on the shoulder. "I will see you in the Valley, then. I am sorry. It is the most I can do for you."

They left me in a cloud of dust. I would have paced, but I knew my knee would buckle. Instead, I prayed. Once I would have prayed in confidence. I sent them up to a void. I should follow the Arapaho. I had come for them. But how could I teach it to them, if it was a lie?

It would make sense to follow them down the mountain. But then, nothing had ever made sense, not since I had met Eithne.

I looked toward the devil's thumb. What would Eithne have done? I chuckled, then sobered.

I followed the Indians down the mountain. I turned my back on the leap of blind faith, chose to walk down the valley once more, instead of climbing the gem-tipped mountain. I did not blame the Arapaho for leaving me behind. I needed the time to think, to familiarize myself with my situation. This gave me that time. I would survive the trip down with the gift of food and medical care.

Once I saw a fox staring at me through a cloud of cold grass. It scampered away, but it shadowed me as I traveled. It comforted me somehow as I hobbled down the shadowed valley.

The shadows deepened. I wearied of my travel and sat down heavily against an aromatic pine. I felt absently for the cross. Its absence pained me. Eithne still had it.

I had braved many dangers to come west. I raised my hand to that lingering smell of lupine tracing its fingers across my cheek, my lifeless fingers touching her sweet scent. Which one of us was more faithless? Who was lying now?

I remembered the stories I had heard as a child about the Indians. Some thought them savage, barbarians incapable of civilized life. Others, a few others, thought them wise. My father had traveled and met Indians himself. He said, "They are people, just like us. They learn our language. They use our tools. They defend themselves, and they have a strong sense of honor. An Indian's identity is found in his tribe. He is part of his tribe like a hand is part of the body."

"But they are like animals," I said.

"And you would be too, if you had been born an Indian."

From then on, I tried to think of the Indians like I thought of the English, or the French—as other people. From that sprouted my desire to tell them the Gospel and share the fruits of democracy. My cousin Angus shared my desire. He was my age. Both of us, twenty and foolhardy. I wondered if I would ever see him again.

The walk down the pass was easier than it had been the way up, and despite what Niwot had said, the Arapaho set up camp every day within my reach. I would walk into camp late evening, meeting their oaken stares, and they would silently share their food. Every evening, too, the medicine man would burn sage while facing the four compass points. Every time he did it, I felt like Eithne would appear. Sometimes I would catch the summery scent of dying flowers and expect her to gambol out of the restlessly swaying pines. She had become as much a part of the land as the rustling corn and black herds of buffalo. Sometimes I wanted her to appear. But then, her fire would leap into my mind and scourge it with doubt.

I was a burden. I knew nothing of living off the land compared with these masters of the plains, the shrewd Arapaho. Each evening, Niwot would give me company. I knew he expected the message I had come to give. But I could never give it. Eithne had borne away my cross.

I performed what services I could silently. Niwot spoke to me on occasion. He was endlessly curious about the lives of the white men.

"This valley is beautiful," he said to me one morning.

"It is very beautiful," I said. The endless fields of gold stretched across the fruited plain, reddened by the sun, like fox hair. The lupine breeze colored the mountains with majesty.

He looked eastward, toward the dawn, and the settlements of the white men. "Its beauty will be its undoing. That is its curse." He looked over the Boulder Valley with a queer half-smile. "You white men. Do you truly wish for peace?" He was a capable thinker, and a curiously eloquent speaker.

Unexpected, coming from a man whose second language was English.

Once, I would have answered immediately, "peace." But once, I had not believed in gods, either. "Some do," I said at last. "Not all. Some hate. Some just want to see blood. Some lie."

He looked up at the mountains, toward the direction of the devil's thumb. "One day, my people will stand on the same peak with your people. We will look at the stars together. Do you hate, Cormac?"

I laughed. But it was bitter. "No."

"Do you lie?"

I pursed my lips. "Yes."

"Then how can I trust that you do not hate?"

He still wore that queer half-smile. I returned it ruefully. "One cannot put his faith on foundations of sand."

He clapped me on the shoulder, chuckling. He said as he went back to the camp, "You are strange. I see now how you captured the fox spirit's heart."

"What?"

But he had already moved into the tepees.

The cold gray mountains sank their toothy maw into the dark, pregnant clouds. The Arapaho slunk in a ragged line down the final stage of the pass, the morning snowflakes nipping the warmth from my cheeks and hands.

They all passed by me, silent, dour as the souls waiting for Charon, gliding away until they crossed the herds of trees.

I stumped onward until evening. My feet ached, my lungs struggled to find air, and my hands could only move like old witch's claws. When at last I saw the Arapaho's fire, I croaked in triumph. I limped past the ring of horses, my eyes cast down to the squelching, freezing mud.

I bumped into a horse. I moved mechanically around it, but it moved with me. Irritated, I placed a hand on it. A foreign hand gripped my wrist. I looked up blearily to discover not a horse, but Kuruk's bear-chest.

I met his gaze, filled with fire. He spoke something in his clicking gibberish, crossing his arms. I knew his intent, if not the meaning of his words. His stance, the predatory gleam—all the same. The saloon, the writhing humanity, and a blue-eyed boy about to die, all flashed before me.

Was this my fate? Every obstacle tripped me, every wall closed in, and all I could do was beat against them with the hands of a feeble scribe, until they took what was most dear to me.

My hands clenched. My brow furrowed. I met his yellowed eyes. My fist connected with his jaw. He staggered back a step. I failed to see the knee which sucked the wind out of me, nor did I see the fist which turned my vision to a thousand glittering stars.

I hunched over, gasping. His hamlike fingers curled on my shoulders. I rammed my head into his stomach. He grunted as his ribs bent.

Pain shot through my back. I tasted grit. My hands sank into the freezing mud and steaming horse manure. I latched onto Kuruk's calf with slippery fingers, pulling with all my meager strength, prying out his weight from under him. He collapsed on top of me, and the stars returned along with a metallic taste.

Kuruk's massive arm wedged between my neck and the sucking mud. My fingers scrabbled to find purchase on his slick skin.

"Is this right?" I grimaced as Kuruk pressed me still further into the mud, my right hand between my windpipe and his bicep. "Is this your justice?"

His hold loosened. I looked up to find the entire tribe watching us. Chief Niwot stood in front of them, his feet as unmovable as the mountain's roots. Kuruk spoke again. Again, his meaning was plain. He does not belong here. He is not one of us. I was a stranger in a strange land.

Niwot, though he remained stock-still, had some effect on Kuruk, for he rolled off me and stood me roughly on my feet. He then led me to a place where I could wash the mud off. The Arapaho looked on, gathering around the campfires.

After I had cleaned myself, Kuruk presented a bowl of pemmican to me grudgingly. My hands locked on the bowl.

Our eyes met. His were a shocking blue. He rubbed his jaw with his free hand and snorted. Then he grinned lopsidedly, shaking his head. Turning his back, he left to sit at his family's fire.

With Eithne's table manners I devoured the pemmican.

I flew across the open grassland. I didn't actually fly. The blessing I had given Alan would deny that power to me for some time. But I could still take an ethereal form. To the animals, to the trees, and to the fields of corn, I was a powerful gust of wind. I barreled across the open miles, toward the South where the Dineh dwelled— White Shell Mountain. I wanted answers. A Dineh medicine man would give me some.

It took me many rises and settings of the moon to find the village. When I did, I watched it for many more. Stalking my prey.

I found the medicine man, and I debated about what to do with him. He was young. The old one accompanied him, teaching the traditions the Dineh favored for healing. He stank of Coyote. If he didn't know the answers, I would have to find another who stank just as badly.

He had been very careful. He used his paltry blessing to erect a spiritual barrier about the village. It posed no threat to me, but I would have to revert to my human form to cross it. I smiled. I could have some fun with that.

Night fell. The Dineh retreated to their hogans. I changed behind a dead tree, clothing myself in fox skin—not real fox skin. I would never slay the animals I guarded, and I was glad not to have to make use of a dead one. I made an illusion. If someone touched it, they would feel nothing. But they wouldn't want to touch me. I had become one of the Dineh's worst nightmares. A Skinwalker.

I turned about, studying myself. The moon would make my eyes blaze. The fox skin would redden my own skin, giving me an aura of blood. Coupled with my teeth and claws…well.

The hogans squatted in a wide plain. Few trees sprouted. I crept forward, taking care not to disturb the brush and alert them to my presence.

I passed the first hogan. The sleeping family breathed deeply. In front of my prey's house was a dog, eyes drooping. It looked a lot like a coyote, mangy and cruel.

I tackled it, snapping its jaws shut before it could warn its master. I sent it to sleep with a tap on its forehead and licked my lips in anticipation.

The prey's hogan was dark. I saw him, sleeping alone, surrounded with woven blankets. Charms against evil decorated him and his hut. I smelled ash near the entrance. I didn't worry about such contrivances. They were used to keep the real Skinwalkers out.

From my stalking, I had gathered his name was Yanisin. In his tongue, his name meant "ashamed." As he should be for hunting alongside the Trickster.

I whispered his name into the darkness. He rolled, but slept on. I whispered again. His charms clinked and rustled. He blinked. I pounced, clamping my hand over his mouth.

He heaved under me like a panicked rabbit. I lowered my teeth to his ear. "I smell Coyote."

He froze, still breathing hard. I licked his ear and snapped my teeth. He squirmed. I held him fast with my god-strength. "I have questions for you."

He looked me in the eye, then away, avoiding my hypnotic gaze.

"You have an agreement with Coyote. What is it?"

He growled. I chuckled. "Struggling will only make it more painful for you."

His eyes shined with defiance. I banged his head on the ground. His eyes watered. He groaned. "Now, will you answer me, or will I have to pick it from your brains?"

He muttered. I removed my hand from his mouth. "I'm only doing what is right for the Dineh," he spat.

"I don't care about your reasons."

"I killed a white man."

"Wh…What?" Not the answer I expected. What did killing a white man have to do with me?

"I killed a white man, and stole a paper from him. I gave it to Coyote."

"A letter?"

"Yes, a letter."

"Did you know the name of this man?" A terrible suspicion creeped up my spine.

"No."

"How long ago?"

"Three seasons."

Alan had mentioned a cousin. So…this man had killed him. Though I did not know his name, even now I smelled the last lingering bloodstains of Cormac. Coyote had sent that letter to Alan, luring him to the white man's fort…Bent's Fort. Unknowingly I had rescued him. My promise to him bound me more than the bond between men. It reached to the mountain's roots, to the primal bonds which joined the world and gods.

Coyote had outfoxed me, sent me away thinking I was his prey. He had even tricked Mother!

I blew out of the hogan, caving it in. I didn't know what the Trickster wanted, but I couldn't let him have it. Alan was *my* prey.

It had been two weeks since Eithne had left me with the Arapaho. Sunlight splashed over the Boulder Valley, illuminating the last vestiges of the dying aspen leaves and the dark green of the eternal pines. Clouds bloomed in the deep blue sky like vast roses.

Chief Niwot sat with me this morning. "Your people truly hold people against their will, and force them to work for you without conquering them?"

"They were never conquered. It is simply the way it has always been."

"This war your people fight is to free them? Were they people of your nation?"

"They were never people at all, at least not to some. It is complex, but I think for most people the war is about keeping the Union together."

Niwot stroked his chin. "This is strange to me."

"Many of your customs are strange to me as well."

He nodded. With an eye sharp as an eagle's he surveyed the Boulder Valley. "I will tell you a story." He pointed across the plain. "Look there." A small shape bounded through the tall grass. "It is a coyote chasing a hare."

With a start, I glimpsed the coyote's gleaming eyes. Niwot ignored or did not notice my discomfort. "One day, Coyote caught Hare. Hare cried, 'Coyote, do not eat me, I have something important you must hear.'

Coyote allowed Hare to sit at the entrance to his house. Hare said, 'I am very much afraid of people. When they see me they aim arrows and I tremble!' With his trembling he caught Coyote off guard. Hare dashed away into a house made of stone. Coyote could not destroy the house.

Hare asked, "How will you kill me?"

Coyote said, "I will kill you with fire."

"What will you set the fire with?" Hare said. "The grass is my food. It will not kill me. The trees will not either; they all know me."

Coyote said, "I will bring the gum of the pinyon and set fire to that."

"Now I am afraid," Hare said. "Pinyon is not my friend."

Rejoicing, Coyote brought all the gum he could carry and set fire to it at the front of Hare's house. The gum boiled like hot grease, and Hare cried, "What shall I do?" But he knew this whole time what he would do. "You are so close you are blowing the fire on me and I will soon be burned!" he said. Coyote was so happy at Hare's fright that he drew closer and blew harder. Then Hare suddenly threw the boiling gum into Coyote's face and escaped.

"It took Coyote a long time to remove the gum. That is how he realized how stupid he was."

Niwot leaned back and sighed, content with the sun warming him.

"That is not my experience of coyotes," I said. "They are despicable creatures."

Niwot cracked one eye open. "Coyote is not despicable. The earth needs him like it needs the buffalo, or the deer. I pity Coyote for his cruelty."

Another sight on the plains caught his attention. "Chief Black Kettle is here."

A large group of Indians was moving our way. I estimated their group to be at least two hundred. "Are they friendly?"

Niwot smiled. I interpreted that as a yes.

The size of the Indian village grew threefold in a single day with the arrival of the Cheyenne. Chief Black Kettle and Chief Niwot got along famously, going about the village together with a certain gregarious aplomb. I passed Kuruk entertaining the company of a number of other young men, but I thought it best not to linger and ducked into the tepee I shared with the medicine man. I stayed there until evening. I decided it would be best to keep myself away until the Indians had settled themselves down. However, they did not quiet until the sun had long since set.

I had gone to relieve myself. It was a burdensome task with my crutch, so I took my time coming back from the latrine.

At this point, most of the Indians had gathered about the central bonfire, but three furtive shapes raced between the tepees. It was Kuruk and two strapping Cheyenne men.

I slid behind a tepee. They slunk past without noticing me, heading toward the edge of the camp. Likely up to some mischief. I decided it would be best to distance myself, so I went back to the medicine man's tent as if I had seen nothing. I lay down on the warm bedding and sank into slumber.

"Niiteheibi! Niiteheibi!"

The cries jerked me from my slumber. I rubbed my eyes. A rooster cawed, sounding like it was dying. Was it morning already? The medicine man still snored…

I rolled out of my bedding and peeked outside the tepee. The moonlight's rays shone dimly upon a large, lumpy figure…two figures. Two men. One dragging the other along on his shoulders.

Kuruk.

I limped out of the tepee. "What happened?"

Kuruk was screaming in pain. That was the sound I had mistaken for a rooster. I limped beside them and took his other arm. We struggled to get him to the medicine man's tent.

The flaps opened and the medicine man peeked out. He saw us, and without a questioning word propped the flap open and motioned us inside. We laid Kuruk down on a wooden bench. My shirt stuck to Kuruk's side. It came away dark and sticky.

The medicine man spoke a command to the other one. He darted out of the tepee.

The healer lit a candle. Kuruk's side bled profusely from a small, neatly shaped hole. A bullet wound, I guessed. I turned away to keep from retching.

The medicine man busied himself with cleaning Kuruk's wound. Footsteps at the door diverted my attention from Kuruk's screams of agony. Chief Niwot ducked into the tepee. His countenance was grim as he surveyed the young man. He knelt down by Kuruk's side. Painful and gurgling conversation followed. With every word, Niwot's expression grew darker.

The medicine man rattled through his store of herbs. "What happened?" I asked.

"He and two others tried to raid a white family's home." Niwot's hands clenched on the folds in his clothing. "The fool brought about the death of a Cheyenne kinsman."

A word from the medicine man stopped Niwot. They chattered together. The medicine man was gesturing to his supplies. Niwot gestured with a wide arm sweep as he responded. I gathered that an essential healing herb had gone missing.

Something nudged my hand. I looked down, and nearly lost my skin from fright. A fox stared up at me with slanted brown eyes.

I looked up at the two men. They were too busy rooting about in the medicine man's stores. I looked at the fox once more. It stared at me expectantly, bobbing its head. In its jaws were leaves of some kind. It spat them on the ground and cocked its head at me. I mimicked it. I wondered if I might be hallucinating.

It bobbed its head at the leaves, then met my eyes again. It nudged the leaves toward me. Bemused, I gathered the leaves. It bobbed its head toward Kuruk, then dashed out of the tepee.

"Excuse me," I said to Niwot and the healer. "Is this what you are looking for?"

Both of them stared first at me, then at my proffered offering of plant detritus. The medicine man swooped on me and scooped it out of my hand. He bent over Kuruk once more.

"It is not enough," Niwot said.

A cold snout nudged my hand again. "Here." I shoved the fox's offering into Niwot's hands.

"Where are you—" Niwot began, but a choked gurgle from Kuruk distracted him. The injured Indian thrashed wildly, forcing Niwot to help the medicine man hold him down. By the time Kuruk had calmed, the fox had returned. Niwot caught a glimpse of it as it deposited more herbs into my hands. His eyebrows rose. I shrugged helplessly and gave him the fox's gift.

Kuruk calmed as the hours passed, whether from healing or the slow slipping away of his soul, I could not tell. Its work had finished with the fetching of the first herbs, but the fox stayed with me through the night. The fox disappeared soon before sunrise.

With the sunrise I left the tent to sit outside. Chief Niwot soon joined me. We watched the dawn together, the golden rays spilling over acres of cold, dry plains. "He will live," Niwot said. "He will not hunt for many days, but he will live."

Niwot frowned, his rugged, weathered lines stretching about his jowls. "He told me he killed a white man." His gaze fell to the ground, where the leaves swirled about his feet. "The fool does not realize what he has done. We have worked so long for the peace we have, and even this peace may shatter like thin ice on a stream."

I nodded. There were no words of comfort or advice I could offer. The best I could offer was an ear.

"Thank you, Cormac."

"For what?"

"Capturing the fox spirit's heart."

"You said that before. What does that mean?"

"I think it means good fortune for you."

Niwot left. I remained to watch the golden sunrise.

Word spread of the miracle of the fox. The Cheyenne and Arapaho treated me afterward with deference, even reverence. Where once someone would bring me food, now they invited me to their fires. Though we did not speak each other's tongues, they seemed content to include me in their circles. One woman, whom I later learned was Kuruk's mother, gave me a hide shirt and a pair of moccasins, for which I was grateful, as my current clothing had become quite worn. For my part, I remained bemused. I continually protested that I had done nothing. The Indians, however, seemed determined to turn it into a legend.

Kuruk was a restless patient. He endured the medicine man's treatments with a martyred expression. At last, someone brought him a sturdy stick to whittle. His work left him covered in shavings.

A week after he had been injured, he was allowed to walk. I saw him exit the tent one afternoon, his stick in hand. He saw me. "Cormac."

I came to him. He pressed the stick into my hand. It was sturdy, about the size and shape of a cane. Kuruk had whittled the likeness of an eagle's head on the handle.

"Thank you," I said haltingly in the Arapaho's speech.

"Thank you," he said in English.

We went about our business. He returned to his family, and I stumped about with his cane.

Chapter 7

"Chief Black Kettle has put up the flag."

I looked up at the American flag flying over the Chief's teepee. They had been told this would show their peaceful intentions. More roving tribes had joined us. Our camp had swelled to nearly a thousand, though the chiefs had sent most of the men out hunting. Additionally, they had forbade the Dog Soldiers anywhere near Sand Creek. Only women, children, and the elderly and infirm camped here.

Emissaries from the Colorado government had arrived over the last week to discuss a meeting with the Indian chiefs. I had stayed out of the proceedings. I could not speak for either Indian or white man. I was just a stranger from New York.

They had obeyed the messenger's instructions to the letter. Black Kettle and Niwot were inside the teepee, discussing how they would negotiate further terms of peace.

I looked out over the plain, toward the Colorado Territory militia. The plain was red with the new dawn, the light spilling and pooling over the prairie. I had never participated in a peace treaty negotiation, but I thought it odd that the militia had armed themselves. I banished the thought, sending it with the flurries of dead grass and leaves. These were, after all, Indians. Until I had spent my time with them, I had thought them savages as well. Still thought them savage, but only because they had no luxury to be otherwise. I wished I could do more to bring them the benefits of the east. Perhaps I could ask Left-Hand if I could sit in on the meeting, to ease the fears of my countrymen.

Chief Niwot emerged from the teepee, looking sober. I watched him merge with the Cheyenne and Arapaho womenfolk, talking with them. He tickled a child, and asked Kuruk's mother about his condition. He was a man, like any other man.

I had come West with my own prejudices, not realizing how foolish they were. I was glad to know the Indians were not all as evil as the stories suggested. Glad to be on friendly terms with them, though I had done nothing to deserve it, I regarded them as equals.

Eithne's features swam before me. I had not been very accommodating to her, either. I had been gentlemanly, certainly, but…not kind. Not understanding. I could not blame her for leaving. Perhaps I could make it up here.

Hoisting myself up with Kuruk's cane, I was about to follow Niwot, when I heard a sound in the distance, a sort of muffled pop. The Indians grew silent, frozen like startled deer. "What is—"

Another pop, from the direction of the militia camp. Another. Soon, a cascade. "They are shooting at us."

Chief Niwot and Black Kettle ran for the pole on which the American flag flew. They raised a white flag. "Why do they shoot at us?" Black Kettle said. "We came here in peace!"

A thunderous boom shook the ground. The earth exploded beneath me and hurled me into a tepee. Stars and darkness whirled before my eyes. It took a moment to come to my senses, to discern the shapes around me. Women and children, fleeing.

A woman cowered in front of me. I shook my head, crawled, helped her stand. "Run!" I yelled to her. My voice vibrated silently in my throat. Terrified, she bolted. Others ran past us, screaming, wailing, dying in ringing silence. The woman fell, sprawling. I attempted to help her to her feet, but she rolled over limply. Like a potato sack. A bullet hole, blackly bubbling, in her head.

The sound rushed back. "God," I breathed. The wails of the daughters and mothers. The acrid smell of gunpowder transported me. Running down a dark alley, Eithne at my side.

I might have knelt there forever, transfixed, had a strong hand not clenched my shoulder and forced me to my feet.

"Flee, Cormac!" Chief Niwot pressed against my back, urging me onward. We stumbled through the confusion, through the explosions and hail of gunfire, together. An old Indian struggled with a militiaman holding a rifle and bayonet. His compatriots joined him, spearing the old man through. A tepee, set aflame with the occupants still inside, a child, dashed against a stone. Women, torn apart by cannon fire. And through it all, the sparse, cold, dead fall leaves swirled about their feet. Carrying their souls. How strange, to see leaves on the plains—

A militiaman saw Niwot. He raised his gun. He saw me and his lips quirked. Taking advantage of his confusion, Niwot clubbed him over the head with a vengeful fist.

As Niwot stood over the man, his gaze raked the gory spectacle before him. He screamed something in Indian—a war cry—and flung his arms wide. He wailed as his people, his sons and daughters, watered the earth with their blood.

I stumbled over the dead and dying, over people who reached their bleeding hands to me, begging for help, for mercy, for release. They fell like leaves around me as I repeated to myself, over and over, "I walk in the valley of the shadow of death, I walk in the valley of the shadow of death, I walk in the valley…"

Niwot seized my hand, and we fled together out of the camp. A gurgling creek stopped our path. The body of Chief White Antelope lay there, face down, his blood seeping down the deathly cold river.

Chief Black Kettle staggered toward us out of the confusion. He held out a hand to Niwot. "My brother," he breathed in his native tongue. Niwot clenched his hand in turn, letting him fall gracefully to his knees. He stared beyond the bloody sun, his soul joining his mourning ancestors in Sheol. Niwot laid a hand on his dead friend's eyes. I met Niwot's eyes. I would remember that gaze forever. It was the gaze of a man who had lost his way. Soulless. A man, dead, carrion. A solitary autumn leaf, whipped about in a gale, already ferried across the river. "They lied to us. What did we do to deserve this?"

Behind him, the hungry, burning eyes of the coyote.

The razor teeth sank into Niwot's shoulder. Niwot screamed. It dragged him back into his burning village. I reached out for him, but I was much too late. For everything.

I stumbled in a daze. The black smoke blew across the red plains. The long brown grass whipped my bloody hands. My cane scraped against the ground. When I finally could bring myself to look back, I found I had not covered much ground at all. "I did not know," I whispered, "that death had undone so many." The coyote's carrion teeth were nowhere in sight, but I knew he was close.

"Alan."

A familiar whisper. "Elizabeth?" The scent of lupine. I turned around. "Is that you?"

I raised my hands in an empty gesture. "Can God feel despair?" A white tear cleaned a path through my blood-flecked face. "Can such rage inflame immortals' hearts?"

She touched my hands. "Alan? What is this? Whose blood is this?"

I blinked. Elizabeth turned into Eithne. But Eithne had gone. She could not be here, not now. She stared behind me, back toward the bloodletting.

"What have you done?"

"I…I'm sorry. I could do nothing."

I knew she would be angry with me. I had failed my end of our bargain.

I reached out. My hand touched her shoulder, grasped for my golden cross about her naked neck. Did hallucinations feel this real?

Fire whirled in her eyes. She howled. The restless grass flattened and bunched like the ruff of a rabid wolf. Dead leaves swirled about her in the chaotic wind. She spoke in a strange language. It rushed like the river, swayed like the stalks of corn, pounced like the stalking fox. I saw her words in the rushing wind, in the blood-red dawn. She spelled out her intent in the red-soaked land.

She tried to brush me aside. I blocked her path.

She snarled and darted. Her claws, lightning quick, gouged my cheek. My blood mingled with the blood of Indians. I caught her arm. Her skin was hot, slick. She slipped from my grasp. I cast my cane aside, wrapped myself around her shoulders, her waist. A stray ball whizzed past my ear. Eithne heaved forward, screaming at the sky. Collapsing, she clawed at the ground.

I gathered her in my arms. My tears, and the blood from the wound she had inflicted, stained her blood-red hair, dulling her golden streaks. Eithne struggled against me, but I took her blows in silence. What words of a mortal man could calm the wrath of a god? What comfort could she find in my embrace? She was one with the land. The blood was her blood. With each death, she died.

Eithne wriggled to face me. I traced the scratch made by the musket ball, fashioned from human hands. She traced the scratch across my cheek, made by hers. Her hand was calloused, careworn. Not a phantom hand. Not an illusion. The fire in her eyes smoldered into embers. Her lips parted. "Let me go."

"I cannot."

"Let me go." Her fire became water.

I touched my palm to the cross still dangling about her neck. "Very well."

She untangled herself from me and the grass. Her soft footsteps scurried away. When I finally emerged from the tall grass, she had vanished.

I did not know how long I lingered. The weather shook me out of my daze. It was overcast. I shivered. Would it rain or snow? Trees. I needed to find trees. For shelter. Should I go to the militia for help?

My lips grew dry at the thought. After what I had seen, I would prefer to die out here. The crows gathered overhead, the spirits of the Furies on their backs, to gorge on the massacre-feast. Some whirled about my head, their raucous caws calling me to sleep.

My body rebelled weakly against this malignant desire. I took up my cane and staggered toward a small, dark wood. When I reached the treeline, I looked for a place to rest. Perhaps that would be best. Just to rest, let myself become one with the land. Forget about everything.

The sticky aroma of the pines calmed me. I had walked in the valley of the shadow of death. I lay down underneath the shadow of an old, dead monarch of the forest. Next to that tree, a rock outcropping, surrounded by brown sticker bushes, protruded out of the land like cold, bony fingers.

I looked up to the dark clouds, framed by the dead branches. My lips moved, though I did not know what I was saying until I decided to listen. "Hallowed be Thy name. Thy Kingdom come, Thy will be done…"

The gods. God, Jesus, Eithne, they were all insane.

Something rustled just beyond my sight in a thick grove of pines. Perhaps a wild animal, come to dispose of my corpse. I had nothing to defend myself with, I realized. Nothing but my cane.

Just as I gave myself up as a meal for a bear, a ragged hat protruded from the brush. Then a leg, an arm, all soiled with pine needles and dirt. They waved about like the crazed arms of a hog-killing crowd. Finally the rotund body and craggy face of Brand appeared. He met my steady gaze.

"So." He shook himself like a dirty dog. "Ye lived."

"Yes." I adjusted myself so I faced him fully. I did not feel surprise, only irony. This was the man who would see me cross the Styx. I recalled something Eithne had said about him, that a trickster had blessed him. "As did you, Brand."

"The pointies 're mine, boy. They ain't killin' me anytime soon." He waddled up beside me. I could not crawl fast enough to get away, so I sat there, composed, as he groaned and collapsed beside me. "Things'll be easier here from now on. I kin guarantee it."

Perhaps he was an illusion then. I hoped so. Easier that way. "I found them. The Arapaho."

"Ye did? Why yew ain't with 'em? They steal yer girl?"

"No…she left. And they are…"

His eyes glinted. "D'ye have any idea where she ran off to?"

My numb heart deafened me to what I said. "I have no idea whatsoever."

"Eh, well." He shifted his bulk, and his eyes darted downward, then back to meet mine. Stalking me. Assessing my weakness. "Makes things easier, that's for sure."

"Makes what easier?"

"Well, you know." He shimmered like a mirage. I blinked and sniffed. "This and that."

His face changed. Gradually, but visibly. He grew thinner. My slowly beating heart skipped a beat. "Are you feeling well?"

"I'm feeling grand, holy man. Just grand."

A chill crawled up my spine. His face was still familiar. He smiled. "What is it, preacher? You feeling all right yourself?"

His voice had become higher. Like that trader's. I adjusted my collar with shaking hands. That horrible sense of irony replaced my longing for death. An illusion? No. It felt like Eithne's presence, yet…wrong. Corrupted. "I am well, thank you."

He scratched his nose. "Yes, everything's just fine. Beautiful. All the pieces in place. The only thing I cannot figure out, is why you left the Creek. I was all prepared to wait another month and a half to get you away from them soldiers. But you came here instead." He leaned forward. "You do not know how hard I have worked to get you out here. First to that old fort, then away from that accursed vixen. That priest in Denver almost had you, too."

I cleared my throat. "What are you talking about? What do you want with me?"

He stretched and laid out on the rock—a languishing beast. "I want you, my boy. You've lied. I have a claim over your life. You also have something I want."

"What is it? Money? I can assure you, I have none." I was jabbering. *God, God, God,* I thought, over and over. *I walk in the valley...*

His cheeks hollowed. His gaze locked on me with a terrible gleaming starvation, a solitary hunger. His smile turned into a desperate grimace. "No. I want your power. I always wanted your power. I almost had it so many times...Now that she's finally out of the way, we can get on friendly terms." He extended his hand. "I am the Coyote."

I took his hand gravely. It was cold and dry, like an old bone in snow. "I am not sure what you are talking about, Brand."

"No, of course you wouldn't." He peered at me with half-lidded eyes. "I am a god."

"I only recognize one deity." But my declaration was hollow. A lie. And he could see through it like glass.

He waved it aside. "Come now, do you still believe that after all you've seen? Do you believe in your invisible god when the true gods of the world stand before you?"

"There are things beyond what we can touch and see." My brain had automatically provided the response, as my other faculties devoted themselves to frantically devising a plan for escape.

"Nothing is out of reach for a god." He sat up and grinned. "I didn't come all this way to debate philosophy. Give me your power."

I was truly confused by what he meant, but I did not show it. "Even if I had any, what makes you think I would give it to you?"

A canine barked in the distance. A coyote? "I suppose I'll just have to eat you." Brand's features changed. His face elongated. His eyes widened, became golden and luminous. His hands morphed into paws. Fur rippled across his skin.

I backed up against the rock outcropping and held Kuruk's cane ready. Pain coursed through my hand. I jerked it back, uttering an oath, or was it a prayer? I had rubbed against a sticker bush. Even if I could run, it would not have been any use. The coyote would have caught me. No fresh tears of terror sprang to my eyes. I had no time for them.

Coyote panted, jaws opening in that familiar smile. It leaped at me, its great jaws sinking into my entire right arm. I screamed, writhed. My blood spurted across my vision. The pain of watching the innocent die, of injustice and cruelty, sank into my flesh.

A flash of golden red streaked across the rocks, bit the coyote, forced him to release me. It placed itself between me and Brand. The fox.

It growled. Coyote glared at it, and moved to swat it away with a massive paw. Then the world exploded. The rocks vibrated with the thunderous boom. I shielded my eyes from the light that had already blinded me. Bewildered, I blinked through the blood and dust.

Two people stood between me and Coyote. One…Eithne. The other was blonde, and wore a white buffalo skin. An owl perched on her shoulder, and a bow rested across her back.

Coyote shrank away, snarling. The blonde woman spoke. But her speech, while I understood it, was not in English. It rustled like the autumn leaves, cracked like lightning, and whispered like the wind. It was as if she spoke the language of nature. "If you wish to devour us now, you are welcome to try."

The coyote slavered, hackles raised. I thought it would attack, but instead, it met my eyes. It seemed begging, beseeching. It turned and loped into the forest.

I gasped. My heart raced. Saved again, by the person I least wanted to see. My vision dimmed. Blood pooled around me...

"Won't moving him higher up the mountain make him bleed more?" Eithne. Distraught. My head lolled. It felt like cotton. Warm hands cradled me. I rocked back and forth in them like a babe.

"I have a chamber. I use it for experiments."

"He'll bleed to death before we get there!"

"Then move faster. We can't linger here. Loki has familiars everywhere."

I reached out with my bandaged arm toward the buffalo skin...

Soft warmth cradled me. I opened my sleep-crusted eyes and looked out to the summer cityscape of New York, framed in voluptuous velvet curtains. My four-poster bed bathed in the sunlight.

"Alan!" My mother, just outside the door. "Alan, get up. The Dawsons are here."

A nervous twinge sent the shakes through me. Today was the day.

I languished in bed for a little longer. It had been an exhausting year. My studies in the Church had worn me to the bone. I had been ready to take the vows that would have made me a full-fledged priest. But, in the end, I was a Cormac. God called all Cormacs to serve in a different way.

My hands shook, and I struggled with the buttons of my shirt. Another knock at the door. "I am coming, mother!"

"Ye are, my boy? Ye seem to be taking a long time to get here." My father, Seamus Cormac, came in, his Irish accent dancing a melodious jig. I had not adopted the accent.

He helped me with my last button and looked me over steadily. "Ye'll be fine." But I saw the longing in his eyes. The same longing I had in my heart. My father had never been able to take the priestly vows, either, and his father before him. Our family had lived a lie since time immemorial.

I walked down the long hallway, filled with great works of art, familiar to me as the picture-books my parents gave me when I was little. I presented myself to Mr. Dawson in the waiting room. He hunched, his beaklike old nose bobbing and black dress coat flapping. "Where is Elizabeth?" I said.

"In the living room. I have some business to attend to with your father. Entertain her while I do, will you?" He stalked into the hall where my father stood in the doorway to his study. Over his shoulder, Seamus locked eyes with me. He gave a small nod. I nodded back. I would do my duty.

I stepped into the living room. Sitting in a plump chair in the opposite corner was Mrs. Finn, the head maid. A fitting chaperone. Her hawkish stare would miss nothing, though her shrewish demeanor could set the whole room on razor's edge.

Elizabeth Dawson stood at the window. The morning sun illuminated her blonde hair. Her light blue dress stood in contrast to the curtains, a delicate tulip in a sea of red. I tried to speak. Cleared my throat, and tried again. Then she turned around and met my eyes. Her sky-blue gaze melted me all over again.

"Alan," she breathed.

"Elizabeth."

She sat on the wide couch next to the window, hugging her knees close. A quaking statue. "I have been thinking about all of this."

"I have as well." If I had moved, I would have fallen over. So I stood next to the door.

"You know why."

"Of course. Trade agreements are important. Especially in America."

"I never wanted this."

She knew I did not want it, either. We had always been friendly, but not overly so. Though I had entertained certain flights of fancy as a boy—the source of my discomfort now.

Her face grew sad. "He only wants your money."

"He can have it."

Elizabeth studied me for a long while. "I do not want you to be forced into this, either."

I knew what would come next. My heart skipped a beat.

"I like you well enough…" She laughed softly, then touched her hand to her forehead. "No, I do love you. I love you enough to go against my father's wishes. Enough to give you what you want. But…I love my father, too."

How cruel her dilemma. This time, I took care not to let my emotions run. "I would not wish to cause problems between you and your father."

She nodded. A colorful mix of emotions played across her face, relief, sorrow, guilt, expectation. I saw beauty in her honesty. I resolved to never hurt her.

"I have something for you." She held a small box in her hand. With her dainty fingers she plucked out the golden chain. On the end, twinkling like the Star of Bethlehem, was a small Celtic cross, beautifully wrought in gold. I saw the sad knowledge in her eyes. She knew what my cousin and I had planned. My lies had laid the truth bare. I could hide nothing. My promise broken before I could give it.

I took out a small box from my pocket. Opening it, I stared at the ring within. This would be my promise to her. Someday, I would come back, even if it was not to marry her. Plucking it out carefully, I offered it to the giant coyote lying on the couch.

I writhed in the soft leather encasing me. "Steady," a voice said. Sweet. Like the tinkling of silver bells.

My breathing slowed. I focused my feverish eyes. A stranger sat beside me, examining my right hand. Light framed her golden hair and twinkled in her gray eyes. I was in a cave. A lamp hung over my head. In the back, just at the edge of the light, there was a solid wooden door.

I groaned. "What happened?"

"You nearly bled to death. You have been unconscious for three days."

I rubbed the sleep from my eyes. "Where are we? Eithne? Is she well?"

"We are underneath the devil's thumb." Her hand left my wrist, and it came back with a damp cloth.

I resisted the urge to pull away. The cloth brushed my forehead. If my skin could have tasted, it would have been ambrosia. I shivered. "There," she said. "That feels more comfortable, does it not?"

I nodded. Feeling drowsy again, I rested my head back on the pillow. Three days? No wonder I felt so wretched. "Who are you?"

"A friend." I was finally able to focus on her properly. Her body, that of a young woman, but her face seemed… strange. Ageless. One second she looked a young girl, the next, as old as time itself. She wore a white buffalo skin, and an owl feather rested behind her right ear. I regarded her with curiosity, and some wariness. "Be at peace, priest. I'm a healer, not a trickster. Or rather, not a malignant trickster."

"Who are you?"

"That is a hard question to answer. Sometimes I am not sure myself."

My drowsiness disappeared in a flash of frustration. I had nearly died. I was not in the mood for dodgy answers. "May I have a name, ma'am?"

"Which one do you want?"

"All of them, if you please."

She winked. Her owl feather quivered. "My name is Athena."

Chapter 8

I took another deep breath. "Say that again."

"I am Athena."

I hid my eyes with my injured hand. I winced when I moved it. Her movements, endowed with unearthly grace, betrayed no subversive intent, only concern. I rubbed my neck nervously. "I apologize for my state," was all I could say. How does one address a god?

"You are no worse than Odysseus when he washed up on the shores of Phaeacia."

"My circumstances feel more like the trials of Jonah than Odysseus. I am no great man."

"Odysseus was more humiliated in his position, but more proud. I harbor no love for proud men. Are you proud, son of Seamus?"

My eyes fell to my hands. "Perhaps I was. Perhaps I was stubborn. Where is Eithne?" The need to see her ached worse than my wounds. So many things to tell her, to explain to her…to apologize for.

"She does not wish to see you."

The discourtesy stung. My temper flared. "She dragged me into and out of hell. Yet she offers no opportunity for me to respond in kind." I was eye to eye with Athena. I did not recall moving there.

I staggered. My wounds throbbed unbearably. The goddess caught me. "You are in no condition, and neither is she."

"Is she all right? She is not injured?"

"No. She is well in body."

My desire to see her drained from me like bees from their hive, to be replaced by a hollow lifeless pain. "I see. Very well."

Athena laid me back down in the bedding. "Rest. Recover. You shall be right as rain in a few weeks. Less, if I have my way."

She walked to the door. "If you need anything, call for me."

The goddess left me to my thoughts. I curled into a ball and waited for sleep to wash away the aches of mortal coil.

I traveled down a long stone corridor, eventually arriving at a homely wooden door. Opening the door, I stepped into Mother's huge reading-den. Dried animal hides that smelled of ink, and more recently, thin sheets that smelled like wood and bound in blocks, lined shelves carved into the stone. It smelled like old dry logs. A fire burned merrily in a hearth in the middle of the room, surrounded by wooden chairs and a small table. Mother sat there, the fire's reflections dancing across her cotton white robes and in her gray eyes. She had already buried her nose in a book with many pages. A cup filled with an aromatic drink sat on the side-table.

Mother looked up as I entered. "So," She rested her elbow on the table, and her chin in her hand. "Do you care to explain your actions to me, or shall I divine them myself?"

"What do you mean?"

Her eyes strayed back to the book. "Do you truly mean for me to guess?"

I sat in a chair opposite her. The fire between us crackled, and the hole in the ceiling sucked up the smoke. "I don't know what you mean."

"You have never taken such interest in a human before."

"I made a promise that I would guide him and translate for him. Guiding him includes protection. I don't break promises."

Mother raised her eyebrows. "You have never taken the time to know one. Why now? Why in this way? You have stepped over the line. I should punish you."

I growled. It came out as more of a gurgle.

"You know the laws."

I scuffed the floor with my footpaw. She continued. "You save him from Dineh raiders. You follow him, and offer him your services. You save him from the Trickster. If you had done this two hundred years ago, I would think you had been switched for a changeling."

"Why aren't you surprised now?"

"Several reasons. Answer me first."

I felt my face redden. My neck became hot. "I'm…not sure." I answered truthfully. I didn't know why Alan drew me. Why I kept returning to him, like some tame dog.

"Would you like to know why?"

I looked at her, really looked, since the first time I had seen her in the forest. She had never looked old, but her aura felt old. Her body, immortal, but her spirit aging. She seemed worn, almost decayed. "Can you untangle this burr?"

She settled herself into her chair. "It's love, Eithne."

I recoiled. "I don't love him."

"Does it not feel familiar? Do you not feel the bond you made with him when you saved his life?"

My breath rattled out like the leaves on the wind. "Why, if it is love, would I feel it now?"

Athena tapped her lip with a finger. "We become gods over that which we love most. We exist to guard the world. Each of us is given a task, a duty. You manage corn, beans and squash. I oversee human knowledge and wisdom. The one thing we were never given control over is human will. Have you ever loved a human? A man?"

"What use is love to me now?" If Mother had any sense of justice, she would leave me be. Leave me to become one with the earth.

"The choice itself means something, Eithne. Have you noticed how hard your work has become?"

My eyes wandered listlessly about the room. I wasn't sure how these related, but I answered anyway. "It has become…difficult. I have to concentrate more."

"What is difficult for you, is now almost impossible for me."

"But…" My brow furrowed. "That doesn't make sense. If the humans have increased in knowledge, then wouldn't your gift increase as well?"

Mother passed a weary hand over her eyes. "It started with the Greeks. They needed me less and less, and so my power over them decreased. The Romans made it worse for all of us, except briefly toward the end. The Christians—they were the worst of all. They denied us completely. When the Europeans came, they pushed us away with their unbelief…No. They wanted power over the world. Science has replaced me. Something greater than us behind the Europeans is pushing us, taking over tasks that were once ours alone. Perhaps it is the humans themselves. Perhaps it is an invisible god behind them."

"An invisible god?" Alan's talk of his god, Jesus, came back to me. The thought made me squirm.

"I safeguard human wisdom, which deals with the natural world. I would not know of something outside the natural realm, not with any certainty. There is a possibility of a god beyond, even above, us. Don't you see? Our love for humanity damns us. As they grow, we wither. But your love for him and his love for you…who knows what might happen?"

The discussion reached into dark places. Scary places. "I told you I do not love him!'

"I have a theory." She paused. I had never seen her hesitate to give information before. The always knew what to say, what to do. "You're not going to like it."

I braced myself.

"I think we used to be human."

I blinked. "What?"

Mother clasped her hands together. "You've felt the terrible loneliness of the void our voices have left behind. For thousands of years we hated each other, but our songs never faltered."

My hackles rose. Horror clawed at my belly. "I don't believe you."

"There is more. Some gods have not disappeared outright. The power they held never leaves our awareness. It…melds. It combines with other waning powers."

"One waning power is Coyote. Loki. The trickster god." She smiled wryly. "It makes sense, when you think about it. Mankind has mastered trickery, so the first of us to be set adrift would be the trickster. He loved cleverness, but it is easy to love it too much. His desire for Alan's power, though...that is something." She laid her teacup on the side-table. "He has uncovered a terrible secret. He is extending his godhood."

"How does this make us human?" I choked on the question that would have followed: What makes us like Loki?

Mother's gaze, that serenity, made me want to conjure fire. "Do you wonder why you can change into human form?"

I sensed I wouldn't like this line of discussion either. "To talk with the humans if we must, of course."

"Come now, Eithne. The native people of this land can see your godhood." Athena continued on relentlessly as a herd of buffalo. "They understand the messages you breathe through the land. You have no need to change into their form. Answer me this, child. Why can't you change into your god-form instead of your human form?"

I felt numb. But, I had known this. Deep in my heart, I had known.

"It is because we gods were once human."

I shook my head. "I don't believe that."

She cocked an eyebrow. "And why not?"

"We...we're gods. We're better than them. I saw horrible things. I saw them put a youngling to death by hanging him with a rope. They take over my crops, they hunt my foxes…They slaughtered…"

Athena stared at the transparently flickering coals of the fire, dying slowly, their high flame sinking. "Are we better than them? Tell me, what do you think of Prometheus' banishment? Or Loki's suffering at the hands of Odin? No, my dear. We are not better. If anything, we are worse. It proves just how human we are."

My hands turned into claws. I snarled. "I don't believe you." Something wet trickled down my cheek. "I don't believe you!" My snarl turned into a roar.

I snapped, snarled, bit at her, though I couldn't bring myself to actually leap out of my chair and latch onto flesh. How could she endure? What glued her face into that expression of eternal serenity? "Throwing a tantrum will not change the truth, Eithne. Calm down before you wake Alan."

I breathed heavily. My tail lashed, my ears twitched. I collapsed to the floor and curled around myself.

"Is this not further proof? For all our power, we are ugly, depraved. How beautiful humans are, even in their savagery."

"How can you say that?"

"Evil dwells within their hearts, Eithne. But good dwells there also. Think about it from their perspective. If you had been them, you would have done the same."

"You're excusing them? For what they did to the Arapaho? To Alan?"

"Of course not." Mother stood. She paced the floor and sighed. I watched her as the fox watched the wolf. Her feet padded softly on the stone as she traced the corner of one bookshelf. "Everyone does what is right in their own eyes. It is an unfortunate truth. They think they do good when they do evil. If you can overcome this mistake, and look at it from their perspective as well as yours, you will see what I mean." She looked down on me with a compassion that skewered my heart. "Could you have averted this massacre? Yes. But there would have been another. You can't change what they do by force."

"One minute, you sound like you say I mustn't give up on them. The next, you bite your own tail."

She smiled. Smiled! "I'm saying both. Humans can do good and evil in the same action." She reached down to caress my velvet hair. "Your actions still mean something. Behind the world there is purpose. The truth is simply not what you think it was." Her thumb brushed my ear. "Give up your hatred, Eithne. Learn to love. You can't change what humans do. You can only change yourself." She looked me straight in the eye. "Alan is one of them. Would you destroy him as well?"

I dropped my gaze.

When I looked up, Mother had gone. I curled beside the hearth and watched the smoldering embers crumble and blacken.

Chief Niwot faced me. The smoke from the teepees surrounded us. I tried to warn him, to reach out to him. The Coyote—

"No!"

I blinked. I had soaked the pillow with my tears. I dried them on the corner of my blanket. My face felt swollen, my eyes, itchy.

What had been done in the Lord's name? Their faces floated in front of me, a cloud of accusation. I begged for their forgiveness. Their leaves drifted from my hands as I gathered them in vain.

The door to my room creaked. Soft feet padded in. I covered my face in shame. I did not want to see Eithne, not now, not in my distress.

She said nothing. I began to feel awkward with her standing there. At last I peeked out of my covers. I had been mistaken. It was Athena.

We stared at each other. She ended the silence with bedside manner. "How do you feel?"

"Better," I mumbled. A whirlwind of emotions ran through me. Embarrassment. Awe. Curiosity. Trepidation. Athena…goddess of wisdom. Goddess of Odysseus. Could I trust her? Could I believe in her? Did it matter?

I had heard tales of White Buffalo Woman during my time among the Arapaho. She was a benevolent power, but buffalo could kill, even unintentionally.

She sat next to my bedroll. I rolled away from her. She said nothing for a few moments, taking the time to inspect my injured arm. When she spoke again, her voice was soft. "I'm sorry you have become so entangled in this."

She paused, waiting for my reply. I stayed still as a stone. "Eithne has been doing her best to protect you, you know. She wants to help you."

"It does not matter."

"What can I do to help you?"

I considered the question. I did not know why—these gods had never inspired much confidence—but I felt I could trust her. She had a presence Eithne did not. I felt that anything I told her, she would have an answer for. Like any mother would for their child. "I would like to know more about you."

"What about me would you like to know?"

"What legends are true, which ones are false. How the gods came to be."

She told me her story. How she had, long ago, awoken on Mount Olympus, fully grown and aware. How she had nurtured the Greeks and guided their knowledge. How she had nurtured the crafty Odysseus. How the Greeks had eventually been subsumed by the Roman Empire, and how she had become known as Freyja for a time.

"Throughout those times," she said, "I found newborn gods and goddesses who needed my wisdom for their tasks. Eithne was my last pupil."

"Where did she wake up? Where did you find her?"

"You could ask her."

The answer surprised me. "I thought she did not want to see me."

"She doesn't."

"I think it would be best if…"

"You never saw each other again?" She tapped her chin with a long forefinger. "Perhaps. I could take you back to New York if you wish." She raised an eyebrow at my consternation. "Yes, Alan Cormac, I know your city of origin. Some gods have been watching you since your birth."

"Why would the gods care about someone like me? I did not even believe in them until…"

Athena wore a half-smile. "None of us believed you could exist either." Before I could ask her what she meant, she said, "The gods watch over many things. But much is hidden from their sight as well."

A sudden thought, a new question, sent ripples of anxiety through my stomach. "Ha…have you ever seen Jesus?"

Her lips twitched. "Do you doubt your faith, priest?"

My face sunk into my hands. "I do not know anything anymore."

I held myself still, even as my soul writhed. She let me compose myself. When I looked up again, she said, "I never saw him. But I heard of him. I have met many people who started their own religions, many leaders of great nations. But I never met him. He never needed me. None of his true followers ever needed me, either. It seems they have their own wellspring of wisdom to draw upon."

"Are you angry at us for pushing you away, like Eithne seems to be?"

"You are more perceptive than Eithne gives you credit for. No. I am glad. You see, I am man's caretaker. That is a heavy burden. I am happy to pass that on to man."

"What about murdering the Indians?"

She appeared to consider her words carefully. "The Christians make mistakes. So do the Indians. They are human. Evil is a fact, but so is good. But even I do not have all the answers."

Athena stood, her white buffalo robe whisping on the floor. "Now, sleep."

She closed the door behind her.

My injured right arm ached when I awoke that morning, as did my head, though not as painfully as before.

I sat up, rotating my shoulders. This would be the fourth day I had been in bed. I had eaten and drank some yesterday, but I felt as parched as the plains. My stomach gurgled. I felt as hungry as a coyote, I thought with black, cheerless humor.

I looked at my legs, still covered by the thick leathery blanket. Hesitantly, I shuffled the blanket down until I could see my knees. My left was normal. My right had been swathed in a brown poultice. I peeled it off. My knee looked slightly swollen.

I bent it experimentally. It felt like cotton had been wedged in between the joints, but I thought it could support my weight. I rolled until I was on my hands and knees, then cautiously transferred my weight to my left leg. I stood. My right knee complained, but refused to buckle.

I heard footsteps in the hall. Athena strode into the room.

I met her eyes briefly. "Thank you."

She nodded. "Breakfast is waiting for you. You must be hungry."

"Famished."

"I can help you."

"No, thank you. I want to walk on my own."

I tottered out into the hall, Kuruk's cane scraping across the stone. I had never seen beyond my little room. I felt very short of breath, panting heavily with each step.

"The air is thin here," Athena said. "Walk slowly."

"Why? Where am I?"

"You are at the top of a mountain."

The words Chief Niwot had said to me long ago came back. "The devil's thumb?"

"Underneath it."

I nodded.

I made it to the door at the end of the hall. Athena opened the door for me.

Wedged inside the mountain was a small, homey library. Doors poked out from between stone bookshelves. Warm wooden furniture lined every available wall space. A stove, almost a fire pit, squatted in the center. Light filtered in from several wide windows on one side of the ceiling. I pointed to the windows.

She answered my silent question. "I have my own tricks. From the outside, it looks like a mountain face, but I allowed light to flow in unhindered. It is a little complicated to explain."

"Where is the way out?"

She pointed to a ladder in the shadows of the back corner.
"A trapdoor. Disguised. I do not want my studies
interrupted by curious Indians."

I eyed the books and scrolls. "I thought your collection
would be more comprehensive." I had not expected such a
collection in the first place. I was not sure what I had
expected at all.

Athena grinned. A strange expression for such a noble
goddess. Even gods could be proud of their creations, I
supposed. "This is just my reading room. Every door you
see leads to other halls. Every hall has several more doors.
Behind every door is a library that would put your Library
of Congress to shame."

I caught the back of a chair to prevent myself from falling
over. "All of that knowledge in one place…"

"Every ounce of human knowledge to the present day."

I staggered at how much knowledge rested beneath my feet.
I felt surrounded by the eyes of ancient spirits. "I would
like to go outside, I think. For fresh air."

"You wish not to eat yet? Very well. You will need your
coat first." Athena glided away and returned with my
travel-worn garment. Draping it over my shoulders, she
helped me to the ladder she had said led out of this cave.
"Are you sure you can make it up?"

"No."

Athena gripped a chain dangling from beside the ladder. She hauled on it with a very unwomanly grunt, and something groaned from above. A square section of the ceiling lowered toward us. Cool white light filtered down, and with it a flurry of snow.

I watched the platform with interest. It apparently worked via a system of pulleys and gears. Athena had not used any magical means.

The platform lowered to the floor with a low, metallic boom. Grass and snow covered it. I stepped onto it gingerly. Athena followed, tugging on the chain once more. I squinted as my eyes became used to the sunlight.

We came up facing west. The peak sheltered us from most of the wind, but the cold still bit at my unprotected face. The mountain peaks rose all about us, grasping the sky. A lake, frozen over, reflected the gray clouds. Great pine trees swayed in the breeze below, blowing the heady pine scent to the top of the devil's thumb.

I breathed in the icy mountain air. Seeing it made the past few days seem like a dream. I shivered. "How do you keep it warm down there?"

"A vent of hot air from deep inside the mountain warms the stone underneath. That same vent also brings hot water. You will have a hot bath, when you wish for it."

"Quite a luxury for this part of the world."

She gave me a sidelong look. "Eithne still does not bathe, does she?"

I wrinkled my nose. Athena nodded. "I never could get her to bathe."

I looked down the mountainside. I could not face east. The gale was too cold.

"You have been running away for far too long."

I met her eyes. Her face was neutral. "How did you know?"

"Because I am the goddess of wisdom. I know everything about you. I knew it all when I first saw you. I saw your dreams when you slept. I know about Elizabeth. About your desire, and your inability, to take the priestly vows."

Then she also saw the lies I had told to come here. The lies I had told my family, and myself. "I never asked for this."

"Eithne does not blame you."

"Yes she does. I am a monster, like them."

The gray sky mirrored Athena's gray eyes. Only her hair moved. She had become a living statue. "She never asked for it either. She chose it. She chose you."

All of Eithne's actions took on a new light. "She's…"

"No, she is not flighty. Quite the opposite, in fact. Think about how she has kept her promise. She left to protect you, not to abandon you."

She was right. That only made me feel worse. "I left that field of death with no wound. The one drop of blood I left with them, Eithne shed with her own claws."

Athena let her hair fly free in the bitter wind. I felt encased in ice, the wings of Dis stirring the air where leaves, like wisps of straw in glass, bowed and eternally frozen, tumbled to the bottom of Sheol. "She will stay with you until you tell her she has fulfilled her promise."

"And if I tell her to leave me be?"

"She will stay with you anyway. She will safeguard you with every power she has."

I wrapped my coat closer about me. I stamped my foot. My toes had frozen. "What of Coyote?"

"He wants to devour any power he can find."

Coyote's yellow eyes flashed in the pure white snow. "What interest does he have in me?"

"You have your own power, Alan."

"Ridiculous." It had to be. But Coyote had said the same.

Athena raised both of her eyebrows. "Oh? Tell me, then. What attracted Eithne to you in the first place?"

"Whim."

She looked at me sternly.

"Fine. Curiosity."

"In part. But she saved you."

The memory of our first meeting came back to me. She said I had a smell about me, like ripe blueberries. "Suppose I have some kind of power. What is it?"

She peered at me like a seer peering through a foggy crystal ball. "I don't know," she finally said. "How strange. I've never come across a human quite like you before."

Athena turned her gaze back to the mountain peaks. "It seems that whenever the gods come against Christians, we hit a wall. Most Christians do not believe in us at all. Do you believe in God?"

"I am not sure any more."

"I cannot say for certain if Jesus is God. But in all my long years, I can say one thing. There is a higher structure, an order outside myself. Otherwise, wisdom itself can have no objectivity."

I thought about that for awhile. Perhaps. Perhaps I had been wrong. I glanced at Athena. "You look troubled." Was this a good or bad sign? Eithne may be a mystery, but Athena…

"And you look cold."

As we descended, Athena continued to look at me strangely. The platform thumped on the floor. I hobbled to a nearby chair. Athena raised the platform once more. "Why do you insist on skepticism?"

"It is absurd. Impossible."

"You are staring a goddess in the face."

"What power could I have?"

"The same any human has, for a start." She brushed the bookshelves with one hand, cleaning off nonexistent dust. "You are a priest of Jesus. Gods give their priests power. Perhaps he gave you this."

"I am not a priest."

"In your heart you are. That is all that matters." She smiled, though her eyes were downcast. "Ironic, isn't it? That you believe in the unseen, yet don't believe in the seen."

"What should I believe?"

"You decide that." Athena disappeared into an aisle. Her words floated in her silent wake.

I held my head in my hands. My arm throbbed. My knee felt sore. They were nothing, grains in a sea of sand. A sea that threatened to dry me up, leave me a husk.

Athena returned with a savory meal. Seeing me thus, she ruffled my hair. My father had done the same whenever he saw me. I had never felt as alone in my life as I did in that moment, so far away from New York, and in the company of gods. Yet, I could not help but think of how Eithne felt.

Athena knew my thoughts as plainly as if she had written them herself. "Eithne has been alone for a long time. She chose to concern herself merely with the plants and the foxes. But a god is god over what they are most passionate about. She is above all concerned with the freedom to do what is right. The atrocities of the Indians and the Americans pain her more than even you may realize."

Did that mean I had foiled her work as goddess when I had prevented her from interfering in the massacre? Or did that mean I had exercised my own freedom to do what was right in stopping her?

"Do you know why Eithne is so attached to you? At first, the unbearable solitude drove her to seek companionship. She smelled you on the wind, and the scent was pleasing." Athena sniffed. "Yes, like ripe blueberries. The scent of change. She made a promise she should not have made."

"Becoming my translator?"

"No. Saving your life. All gods, especially those like Eithne, are forbidden to involve themselves directly in the affairs of men. The Trojan War proved that to most of us. But it balanced out in the end. Loki, the scavenger of liars, chased you all the way from New York. He meant to kill you himself. Call it providence, call it luck—Eithne nullified Loki's act. She has always been impulsive, and quick to right perceived wrongs."

"How had he involved himself from the beginning? I chose to come out here."

"Tell me, Alan. Do you lie?" I said nothing. Her eyes bored into mine. Whether by a spell or the force of her being, I could not turn away.

Athena closed my fingers around a fork. "Is it right for the gods to hoard such power? It would seem that we were never intended to be immortal. Some wish for more than they were given. Power corrupted us."

"What about you?"

"I have made too many mistakes to be worthy of the power given me." She motioned to the plate she had set beside me. "Come, eat. You will feel better."

Chapter 9

I did as Athena bade me and ate breakfast. It consisted of pancakes, bacon and eggs, with cold chicken. I wondered at the food. A diet of pemmican had sharpened my appetite. I had longed for this. But where had she procured the ingredients? Had she conjured them?

Athena proffered the leftover chicken. "Take this to Eithne. She has not left her room since you arrived."

I almost questioned her wisdom. But I thought better of it. I took the plate mutely.

I limped down the hall to the silent wooden door Athena pointed out to me. The rap of my knuckles echoed against the cold oak with a dismal throb, like a bird rattling inside a cage.

Every breath echoed as I waited. I began to ache. My knee creaked. Perhaps she was asleep. Or she knew I stood outside, waiting for her.

I laid a hand on the smooth oaken face, on which I had expected, hoped for splinters. "Do you think of us as devils?" I whispered to her. I could picture her gray, brooding eyes, the rain dripping down from them, her lithe form twisting in the howling tempest, the terrible, sweet lupine scent as she beat with trembling hands against her fate. "I see now," I said to the faceless door, "that my innocence lay in the weakness of my limbs, not the purity of my heart."

I had collapsed to my knees. With the weight of Atlas, I struggled to my feet and staggered down the hall to my room. I left the plate of chicken at her door. When I returned that way, the plate was empty.

That evening, I stumped restlessly into Athena's reading room. I had half a mind to ask her for a book, but I dithered, uncertain how to ask.

I peered around a bookshelf. Her back was to me, her hand reaching for a top shelf. "Ath—"

Red hair flared and whipped me in the face, and something heavy hit my foot. Eithne swept past me and into the hall, leaving silence in her wake like the plains after a tornado. I picked up the book she had dropped. The title read, *Confessions*.

Pure white caught the corner of my gaze. "You wish for a book?"

"Yes," I answered absently. An odd thought crossed my mind. "Athena, can Eithne read?"

"She is a nature goddess. Of course she cannot read."

"I see…"

She took the book from my hands. "I need your help with something."

Surprised, I met her eyes, then looked away, for her gaze was pain. "What do you need?"

"I need to get Eithne out of her room."

"My help would not be welcome. I think she would rather bite me."

She took my hand and led me down the stone hall. "Trust me."

We stopped in front of Eithne's door. "Eithne," Athena said. "You have to come out sometime."

The door remained firmly shut.

"Stop moping about. It's been four days already."

"What is time to a god?" Eithne's voice was a hoarse whisper.

"I need you to take Alan to soak his leg."

Silence.

"You won't get any more chicken if you—"

"Very well!" Eithne snarled. "I will take him. But that is the last thing I will do for you."

"Good." Athena turned to me. She laid a cool hand across my forehead. "You seem tired. Lay down while we prepare."

I nodded obediently, though I felt no weariness. Eithne followed Athena out of her room, and I returned to my bed to wait.

A breeze stirred my hair, and a noxious scent assailed my nostrils. I sat up and opened my eyes.

The sight which greeted me left me disoriented. I lay next to a pool of bubbling water. Hot steam warmed my hands and the cold air frosted them over. White snow blinded me even under an overcast sky. The lines between sky and land, between water and earth, blurred. Was I dreaming? Or had I awakened? Was it morning or evening?

The pool burbled sweet and tart, overflowing on smooth rock. The pool looked large enough to baptize a horse. A waterfall cascaded over the rock overhang and into the pool. I touched the water experimentally. It felt warm and pleasant, despite its sulfurous smell.

Unable to stand, and still feeling as if I could wake up at any moment, I rolled into the pool, seeking my freedom in its depths. The warmth enveloped me, casting my body to sail through better waters, leaving behind the pitiless sea of my previous life. The sweet sapphire of the morning in the East, gathering in the starlit face of Heaven, filtered through the water. I sang in my mind, the song purging my soul of its sin.

I pushed off the stony, slimy bottom to emerge waist deep in the pool. The breath I took felt like the first breath of paradise, but returning to the real world left me half-encased in ice, so I bowed my head half into the water. No plant which broke out into leaf could long resist even the small waves of this pool. Only grass grew at its edges. This felt like Heaven. But the cold depths of unchanging hell lay a mere arm's length from the edge.

My hands fell about my waist. It felt loose. The belt had fallen off in the pool. It was too worn to support my trousers. In the reflection of the pool I saw the face of a woman. A pure Lady, come from Heaven to guide me up the Mountain at a gentler slope, to where we would both jump off, carried on the wings of an eagle into paradise?

I looked up. Running her hands over the gentle summery tufts of grass, Eithne laid at the side of the pool. Her hair looked like an eagle's roost. Her gray eyes reflected the dull, bare rock. She clearly had not washed herself in only God knew how long. But around her, and around the pool, the grass sprang up as if it had always been summer—a circle of life, slowly spreading wider to the other hot spring pools.

"Hello Eithne," I said.

Her eyes flicked, but remained unfocused. She was listening. Now, if only I could determine what I wished to say. I started again. "It has been a long time."

She twirled a bit of grass about her finger.

"Thank you."

Her ear twitched. "For what?"

"The fox."

"Oh."

"It saved my life."

"Did it?"

"Before you and Athena saved me from Coyote. It distracted him. It helped me in other ways as well. It fetched herbs for a dying Arapaho."

She hid her face. Her next words came muffled in dirt. "What was his name?"

"Kuruk." I spotted my cane on the pool's edge. "He gave that to me."

"Kuruk. The bear. He was a warrior. Impulsive."

"I fought with him. I bloodied his nose, I think. He seemed to like me after that."

I could not tell whether Eithne's noises were laughs or sobs, but she stilled soon after. I waded to the edge of the pool where she lay. "Eithne, could you please look at me?"

"Why?"

"I wish to tell you something, and I want to see you while I say it."

She peeked from between the grass stalks. I took a deep breath. "For everything I have done, and everything I have not done, I ask your forgiveness. None of this would have happened, had I…"

Had I what? Not wished to evangelize the Arapaho? Had I not left Elizabeth?

Eithne sat up. "You think it's your fault?" Her lip curled. "You had no power over them. You never did." She tore a clump of grass up by the roots. "Did you bring them to the creek? Did you load the thunder-sticks?"

"No. I failed my end of our bargain."

Her eyes narrowed. "What?"

"I could not teach them about Jesus."

She laughed. The sound had a cruel edge. "That is seeds on the wind." She crept on all fours toward me. "Who cares for the land they lived on?" Her hand gripped the edge of the pool. "Who failed to see the Coyote's trap?" Her voice rose. "When the thunder boomed and the lightning struck, who failed to come to them?"

"I did." I stretched out my hand.

"I could have brushed you away. I was weak. I never should have saved you." She had grown livid. Her gray gaze stared into black depths. "I should have seen this coming. I could have wiped away all white men as they came ashore. But I wanted peace. Mother wanted peace." I rested my hands on her shoulders, her face, stained black with the smoke of her dying people, inches from mine. She was looking west. We could not see it, but I knew she looked toward the devil's thumb. "Can my people ever stand on the same peak with your people? Can we look at the stars together?"

She trembled like a mouse. This strong woman, this goddess who had lived a thousand years, could only tremble now. A silvery trail parted the dust on her cheek. I wiped it away, discovering the color the smoke had bleared. I would take the first steps toward forgiveness, to mercy, now, with her. "The tears of a god are precious."

I scooped a handful of the sulfurous healing water. With a light touch, I washed her face of hell's grime, and all its dust. Eithne's lupine scent overpowered the smell of the water.

"I knew how evil men could be. Why was I surprised at this?"

I bathed her head in the warm water, washing her hair, ridding it of dirt, combing out the tangles with my fingers.

"I failed in my task."

My hands could not finish this work. Someone with stronger limbs would have to right this. "My knee feels better," I said. "I think I shall come out now." The air had become warm. The curious extension of life had spread out until the snow's edge could only be seen on the next hillside. It was an island of summer in the sea of winter.

I heaved myself out of the pool. I could not rise to my feet. My trousers slipped. "Let me fix that," Eithne said. She plucked long strands of grass and braided them together speedily as I dried myself in the sunlight peeking through the dispersing clouds. Each strand grew back as she plucked them. "What time is it?" I asked.

"Morning." Eithne circled my waist with the new belt.

"Is this a dream?" The world went in and out of focus, like one of those new-fangled cameras. I closed my eyes and breathed in the fragrance of the soft earth.

When I returned next to the world of the living, I found myself in the room where Athena had taken care of me these past several days. The smell of sulfur lingered in my nostrils as I stood up laboriously with Kuruk's cane.

I went out to Athena's study. The gray-eyed goddess seemed to know I would appear at that moment. "Did you sleep well?"

"I did."

"How is your knee?"

"Better. Much better."

Eithne appeared from around an aisle, holding a book upside-down. She growled at it and raised it above her head.

Athena's hand shot out and latched onto Eithne's wrist. "I have a suggestion, Alan. Why don't you teach Eithne to learn how to read?"

I raised my eyebrows. "What?"

Teaching Eithne was like teaching a two-year old with a severe overdose of sweets. I had failed dismally at teaching her manners. I had even said so to Athena. But she insisted. "She has little knowledge of Homer or Dante. Eithne will continue trying to read until she tears apart my library. I can't have that happen. Stop moping about, and do something useful."

The last part stung. "I haven't been moping."

"Yes, you have, and so has Eithne. It's getting on my nerves. So, I'll give you both something to do."

I grumbled.

"Would you rather copy out Plutarch's *Lives*? I have an extraordinary amount of copy work."

"Very well," I said stiffly. "I will teach Eithne to read." It would pass the time at least.

The next morning Athena produced a chalkboard and chalk. I wrote the alphabet, majuscule and miniscule, out on the top of the chalkboard.

Eithne attempted to look disinterested, but her eyes followed my movements. Athena had forbidden her to return to her room.

"This is the letter A." I traced a capital A on the space below my alphabet. Eithne sat at a desk Athena had procured. Her head first cocked one way, then the other. I felt like the recipient of a wolf's curious gaze. I continued, though the image lodged in the back of my head, tempting me to frivolity. "A is for apple."

I wrote "apple." "When you read the letter, it makes one of two sounds—"ah," as in apple, or "ei," as in ape."

"So each letter pairs with a sound."

"Exactly. Now, you'll be interested to know that in ancient Greece…"

Eithne's eyes glazed over. Perhaps I was getting into too much detail.

"How many letters are there?"

"Twenty six."

"Do I have to learn all of them? I could learn to read with only a few, couldn't I?"

"No. You need all the letters." I turned back to the board, erasing "apple," and writing a capital B.

"What about the letter after A?"

Confused, I replied, "This is the letter after A."

"No, there's a small one after it." She pointed to the miniscule "a" beside the capital.

"That is also the letter A."

"But you said the other one is A. How can two different things be the same letter?"

"Capital letters begin a sentence. The small form of A is used everywhere else."

"What's a sentence?"

"This is a sentence." I wrote out "The cat is fat" on my chalkboard.

She peered at it for awhile. "So there are really fifty-two letters."

"No. Each big one is only used at the beginning of a sentence." A brilliant simile popped into my head. "Think of it like a caterpillar. It is also a butterfly. They are the same, but not the same."

Perhaps it was not very brilliant, or even very clear. However, she seemed to grasp it. "I see. The next letter, then."

I turned back to the chalkboard, swiping the chalk from Eithne's hand as I did. "B is for boat." I wrote "boat."

"What's a boat?"

I ground my teeth. "The thing humans use to cross water." I drew a simple boat on the board to give her an idea.

"Like what you used on the lake-river?"

"Yes, like that." I had forgotten she had stalked me since the Mississippi.

"But where are the wheels, and that metal trunk that sticks up from the middle?"

"Paddle-wheels and smokestacks? Most boats do not have those."

She narrowed her eyes, peering at me skeptically. "Why did you use that as an example, then? How am I supposed to know what most boats look like?"

"I did not, you did. I mean…You are getting off the subject!"

She rested her chin in her hand. "Are you sure you know what you're doing?"

I lost my temper. I threw the chalk at the board. It ricocheted off, hitting Eithne in between the eyes. She reeled back, arms and legs flailing. She glared at me from her tangled heap.

I laughed to hide my shame at giving into anger. Eithne gathered herself on all fours, murderous intent in her eyes. I took a step back. "Hang on a moment—"

She tackled me, hissing in my face as I hit the floor. I struggled against her, managing to keep my left arm from being pinned. I briefly wondered at that, for she had thrown men much stronger and heavier than me.

She raised the offending chalk. I shielded my face. She tore my arm away. I winced in preparation for her vengeance.

I felt a light tap on my forehead. Opening my eyes, I saw Eithne's triumphant grin.

"This doesn't look much like reading."

Eithne scrambled off me. I stood up laboriously. Eithne had avoided my injuries somehow, for which I was grateful. My face grew hot with embarrassment. Athena tapped her chin with some rolled paper, staring at Eithne.

Eithne's eyed darted to and from Athena's. She looked like a child with her hand caught in the cake. I tried to understand the exchange. In the end, the gods, especially women, eluded my understanding.

I cleared my throat. Athena shifted her weighty stare to me. I caught a glimpse of amusement there before my own eyes dropped. Who would have thought a legend such as Athena would have a sense of humor? Or a kindness unrivalled in the hearts of men?

I cleared my throat again. "Ahem, well, we must get on with the lesson."

After that, we steadily achieved progress. I found, to my surprise, a keen awareness and understanding behind Eithne's seemingly random questions. Eithne was curious about everything—at least, everything she asked about. If I tried to interject an explanation on something pertaining to my own interest, her eyes glazed over. But she learned. I was not certain why she felt so motivated, but her determination made it easier.

Over the next several days, I taught her the basic structure of English. She was writing basic sentences by the end of the second day. She learned particularly well when she spoke what she read. Her grasp of the language astounded me. She was almost like the Eithne I had known before all of this god-madness. Athena caught one of my looks of amazement. She remarked, "Think how many languages Eithne has had to master over the ages. She's learning a language she knows already in a different form. It's easy for her."

Athena interrupted us one evening. "You both must be famished by now. I've prepared a meal for you." I dropped my chalk while writing John 20:29 from memory.

I caught a whiff of delicious, mouth-watering…

"Chicken!" Eithne exclaimed. She burst past me, only for Athena to stop her mid-stride. She growled.

"Stop running in my halls," Athena said.

Eithne's lip curled. She stumped around her and toward her room, flinging the book she had been attempting to read over her shoulder. St. Augustine's *Confessions* hit me squarely in the forehead.

I had always found women utterly confusing. To a degree, terrifying. Eithne was the most baffling woman I had ever met. One moment, I thought we had settled on friendly terms, the next, she threw a book at me. How had I decided on her as a traveling companion?

And yet, I had trusted her initially. Her behavior thus far had eroded that trust. But she had saved me on the mountain pass, and that had thrown things into even more confusion. She had turned into the thing she had said she was all along. A goddess. A being, hundreds of years old. And she had led me to Athena, the goddess of wisdom and war.

I never expected it to feel so…normal. I sat at a dining table wedged between bookshelves, breathing in the aroma of chicken and dumplings. Where did Athena get all of these things?

Athena swept into the cramped space. Surprised, I stood, remembering my manners. Athena cocked her head. I realized where Eithne had picked up the habit.

"What are you doing?"

"Ah…standing."

"Why?"

"It is polite in the presence of women."

"So you do think me a woman."

Was she pleased or angry? "If I remember my myths correctly, the gods are similar to mankind in many respects."

"Indeed." Gray-eyed Athena looked at the spread, then at her bookshelves. "Come with me for a moment. I wish to show you something."

I followed her to the elevator outside. We rose into the chill mountain air. The night was cool and clear. A nearly-full moon, silvery-white and clear, made Athena's buffalo skin glow.

Athena sighed heavily. It was as if the moon rested on her shoulders. Could gods become weary?

I thought back to when she had told me she knew everything about me. "It must be a burden to know the things you do."

"Yes. It is." The moon made her eyes shine white. "Do you see the man in the moon?"

It blinded me briefly when I looked at it. "I do."

"That is the face of my brother, Apollo. His just gaze looks down on all of us eternally. But even the moon waxes and wanes. Even gods must change in the face of unalterable truths. If gods must change, how often must mankind change?"

"Legend says it is also the face of Cain, condemned to perpetually wander after murdering Abel."

Athena nodded. The wind blew a mote of snow into the air, freezing my already cold hands. Athena became like marble. "There is one god who refuses to let go. He has deceived himself into thinking he is unchangeable, immortal. He became the god of lies. He hunts you even now, because he believes those lies."

"How can I be rid of him?" My frozen hands trembled at the mention of Coyote. "How can I stop a god?"

She laid a hand on my chest. "You must change. Loki capitalized on some deceit within you. If you are to have any peace, you must first conquer your lies in here." She retracted her hand and met the moon's shining countenance. "I have a favor to ask."

What sort of favor could I give to the goddess of wisdom? "I will do what I can. What do you need?"

She remained silent for so long, I thought she had gone into a trance. Finally, she said, "I know what your power is, Alan. It took me a long time to discern its nature. Now that I have, I know what I am about to ask you is the right thing to do." She stared at me over her spectacles. "It is a strange power. The gods will bow before it." She looked at me with an expression I never thought would cross her face. It was awe. "Before I tell you, promise me one thing."

I locked eyes with her. "Promise what?"

"Give this to Eithne when the time is right." In her hands she held an olive branch.

"How will I give it to her?"

"What does she love most of all?"

What Eithne loved most of all…was it corn? The foxes? The land?

"Have you seen Eithne's god-form?"

"Her tail? Her ears and claws?"

"Those are attributes. Symbols of her godhood. I am not speaking of those."

"Why did those not show themselves before?" The evening of the shootout, which seemed years ago, came back to me. "I saw them all along. Yet, it seemed I was the only one who could."

"Only one who has been touched by the gods can see their powers. Eithne touched you willingly, knowingly."

"That was very…irresponsible."

"Perhaps. Or perhaps she saw something in you."

How could she see something in me when I could see nothing in myself?

"That is why I ask you if you have seen her true form. It is her most intimate self. We use that form to change the flow of nature. It is the expression of what we love most."

"I have not seen it."

She tapped her finger on her lips. I stared at her, my courtesy forgotten in the sweep of eternity. I was a rat blinking in daylight. A bug, swept into the ocean. A leaf floating on the endless wind. "What is your true form?"

Her gaze shifted from immortal ponderings to me, like the moon giving way to the sun. "What is the face of justice?"

She extended the olive branch to me. I took it. When she let go, it vanished.

Reading these stick-letters was a chore. How could Mother find pleasure in these scribblings? Hunger clawed at my belly. Perhaps it had not been a good idea to forsake eating.

I walked back down the corridor, holding my head in confusion. Maybe food would help me concentrate.

I arrived in Mother's reading room. Before I took another step, I felt something change. Something within the great order of the gods. A violent, swirling thunderstorm that blotted out my sight. It felt as if the great tree holding up the world had fallen, and the powers of the earth had rushed in to take its place.

My vision cleared. I found myself on all four paws. Coyote? Was he here?

I slipped in with the shadows, following the smell of the chicken and of the door to the outside. I smelled nothing unusual. I bit into a chicken breast as I surveyed the dark corners of Mother's reading room.

Mother's contraption boomed. I snarled. Stupid thing, hurting my ears every time it moved. A simple hole would have been better than Mother's constant tinkering.

I slunk back into the shadows. Alan and Mother arrived. Mother showed no alarm. Had she sensed the change? I watched them eat, deigning not to enter their food-circle.

After they left, I curled in front of the fire, intending to stand vigil in case Mother's senses had failed her. I stared at it for several hours, into the evening, until sleep overcame me.

I woke up sometime later. The embers of the fire glowed in the deep darkness of the late night. I realized I was alone.

After dinner I fell asleep almost instantly. Today had been trying…in many ways. It had all come too quickly. I was too overwhelmed to be disturbed by all I now knew.

I woke up to a headache sometime in the middle of the night. I rolled stiffly over. A familiar face greeted me.

My heart jumped. Eithne had snuck in while I slept. Her head rested on the hard stone floor. She breathed slowly and deeply. Her honeyed lupine breath cascaded over my pillow.

Her eye twitched. Her hair had fallen over it, tickling her. I reached over with my left hand and brushed it away. She whimpered.

Her hand met mine. She gripped it firmly. At first I thought she had woken up, but she nuzzled the floor with her cheek. Still dreaming.

I left my hand in her grip. I would not be able to wrest it from her without waking her. I soon fell asleep to her steady breath.

My nightmare tormented me again.

I ran. Arrows pierced me. I crawled to the top of that hill. The yellow eyes in the midst of the villagers.

"Why have you forsaken me?" I cried to the empty sky. The blinding light filled it, and I felt a gentle hand on my forehead.

I gripped it, seeking his comforting warmth, his steady strength. When he fell asleep, I cradled it. I didn't care if he made me feel weak and fragile. I didn't care if he was human.

I woke up before he did. I slipped out and curled next to the fire once more.

I awoke early. The patch of stone next to me lay empty and cold.

I left my room for the study. The morning light filtered through Athena's contrived windows and rested on a huddled shape next to the ashen fire. I walked silently as possible past her toward Athena's elevator.

I looked at it, then at the ladder next to it wistfully. To stand in the free air, if only for a chilling moment…

"Would you like to go up?"

I turned. Eithne stood there, her expression strangely neutral. The light from the newly born sun shone in her gray orbs. "I would," I said. "For a moment."

We rose together into the clear day. For now, the air slumbered, but it would soon wake and rollick its bed of frosted evergreens. A lone crow cawed, alighting on a branch and sending a cascade of snow to the ground. It was different from home. The mountains rested upon the earth like tombstones. Winter here felt like sleep, or death.

The fresh, warm scent of lupine encircled me and heated my chill breath. Eithne gazed out at a land she knew well. She had seen this mountain hideaway in the full bloom of summer. The lake below would have mirrored green instead of white. "It seems so peaceful down there," I said absently.

Eithne followed my eyes. "Would you like to go there?"

"It is too cold."

She took my arm. I warmed immediately. "That is no problem."

She turned to the frozen lake. "Get on my back. I will take you there." I hesitated, my eyes flicking between her and the lake. "Get on with it," she growled.

It would be rude not to take an advantage of such a gesture. Feeling like a child, I clambered onto her back. She was shorter than me. My feet nearly scraped the snow. Kuruk's cane bumped against her elbow.

My hand brushed her neck, and the chain dangling there. She inhaled sharply. "Is something wrong?"

"No. Please try not to touch me as we go down."

I decided it would be best not to point out the absurdity of that request.

Eithne walked to the steep edge of the peak. Fox ears materialized atop her head, tickling my chin. I felt the swish of her tail.

She leaped down the mountain, her strides sure as a goat's, and the carrying of her burden as light as the downy snow. Walking, it would have taken me the whole day to get there. She alighted on the bank of the lake within the hour.

I got off her back. "How strange," I said. "I thought it was winter."

"It is winter," Eithne replied. "Just not here."

"Why?"

"Because I made it so."

The purple lupine rippled in the light breeze. The mirror-calm lake was a shard of sky embedded in the earth. A summery twinkle sparkled from Eithne's neck and in her eyes.

"You still have my cross," I said.

"Would you like it back?"

I could see every detail in her flawless skin. I did not know who had moved us so close. "What would you accept as my atonement?"

"Atonement?" I could see the long seasons in her gray eyes. The lupine wrapped around us both. Her hair was the wind caressing my cheek. Her lips were velvet petals. Her arms, downy fur, her skin, the warm glow of the evening sun. I saw through her eyes, where every moment could be an eternity, and every eternity, a moment. This time, I was the hunter.

Our noses touched. To refuse this would be like refusing the last drop of water to a dying man. This moment felt more real, more tangible, than any moment in my brief flash of existence.

My hand closed on the cross about her neck. Our cheeks brushed.

So, this was what Athena meant. This was why I had to go back.

Eithne stiffened beneath my arms. "What is it?" I asked.

"I smell Coyote."

A trickle of smoke rose from the devil's thumb.

Chapter 10

Coyote. I gnashed my teeth while I bounded up the mountain with Alan on my back. Where was he skulking? He would answer for his betrayal. I would bury him here, then dig him out and feast on his bones.

I alighted on top of the mountain. Alan rolled off me. "Where is the elevator?"

Mother's contraption had sunk back into the mountain. I sniffed the ground. My paw sunk into the earth and closed about a handle. With a great heave, I lifted open the trapdoor. Smoke billowed into the open air, muddling my brain, clearing it of Alan's blueberry scent.

I recoiled, choking. Alan caught me as I fell backward. "What happened?"

"I don't know. The fire down there looks like it's boiling."

"What about Athena?"

"Mother won't fall to a paltry power like this." I raised my nose, breathing deeply to clear the smoke, before falling on all fours. "I must find a way to get to her…"

My vision swam. My head suddenly felt like a cloud of cotton. Something sticky trickled down my ruff…

Eithne's voice trailed away in the billowing smoke. Thickening smoke masked my sight of her. It coated my tongue, dried it until it felt like pemmican. The black smoke whirled about me, a dread thundercloud. It drove me into cleaner air. Could a god die of suffocation?

I fought against the smoke, but it rose like the walls of Jericho. "Eithne! Answer me!"

A muffled shape moved. A bony hand emerged, tendrils of black clinging to its cold flesh. It latched onto my wrist.

I shook my arm like a bull shaking its rider. I fell backward. The hand pulled a body with it, the birth of some demon, ash trailing like twinkling stars. I stared into jaundiced yellow eyes. "There you are, parson!"

I writhed, but he, whipped me over, shoving my face into the hard snow. He pinned my arms behind my back and pressed a hard, freezing object to the back of my head. "If you would kindly stand up," he said, dragging me to my knees. I stood, and he smacked the gun's barrel on my cheek. "You're not getting away now."

"Are you?" I said brazenly. I felt strangely calm. One could only be threatened with death so much.

Eithne rolled out of the smoke. "If you leave now, I will not kill you." She choked, staggered to her feet.

"Brave words for a young pup."

"Or Mother!"

"I don't have to worry about her."

The gun rubbed gently, almost lovingly, against my temple. "You will not kill me," I said.

I could hear his grimace. "So, you believe now? You may have power, but you have proven more trouble than you're worth. I could send you down the river, like I did to your cousin."

My courage drained from me as lifeblood from a slaughtered deer. "You killed him?"

"A Navajo killed him. I simply took the letter off his corpse."

Eithne snarled, but fire leaped up between us. This was no man-made fire. This was god's fire. "Fight me like a god!"

In answer, Coyote cackled. "Give me your power first, and I might."

A bass thump reverberated from the black cloud. A fierce breeze blew away the smoke to reveal Athena, surrounded by a ring of fire. Her hair shone in the morning light. Her gaze had hardened like the tip of a spear. A bow gleamed in her hands. This was not White Buffalo Woman, the wise woman. This was the goddess of Athens, the goddess of wisdom and war. "Loki, you have killed innocents. In return, I have every right to kill you."

"Niwot? Or your brother?" He laughed with the ring of desperation. "What man or god has not lied? What claim is denied me?" Coyote's grip on me tightened. I winced.

Their words echoed dully. Angus. My fault. "Move closer and he dies." I heard the hammer's click.

I expected lightning to strike us, but Athena instead chose to speak. "If you harm him, you will die."

"Perhaps. But then we both lose something, don't we?"

"What do you want?"

"What do I want?" He cackled shrilly. "I want power. That is all I ever wanted."

"You're responsible for the deaths of gods, Loki. Accept your fate."

The gun's muzzle pressed against my head. Eithne stepped forward into the fire, but Athena barred her with a motion of her bow.

"How would you do it then?" Coyote's rancid breath coated the nape of my neck. "How would you keep your purpose? We've become arthritic. When the strength to pursue your calling fades from your limbs, when the call to living becomes a chattering whisper, how would you decide your fate? I followed my desires. I only want what's right for me. He is not even a god!" Coyote raved. "I won't fade away! I won't let the humans take it from me!" His voice grew sly. "Why not a trade?"

No, it was not. It was not my fault. Angus chose his fate. I would choose mine.

"I know better than to make deals with you."

"Come now. I know how much this human means to Eithne."

Eithne bared her teeth. Athena took a step toward us. A step closer to the fire. She grimaced. Coyote jammed the gun into my ear. "I will devour him here and now."

Athena reached out, but withdrew her hand quickly from the hot flames. "The bow. For his life."

The breeze stilled. The fire crackled, waiting to spread. Coyote's grip slackened. "You would trade that? For him?"

"What is that bow, Mother?"

"Not now, Eithne." To Coyote she said, "Let him go first."

Coyote grunted. I panted in the heat from the flames.

Eithne bristled. "Mother, what are you—" She silenced her with a glare.

"Give me the bow."

Athena stroked the wooden shaft. Hefting the heavy stick, she hurled it into the sky. Coyote's eyes followed its graceful arc.

I sank to my knees. The movement caught Coyote by surprise. With every fiber of strength I could muster, I bucked forward, tossing Coyote into the boiling fire. I saw the bow tumble far down the western slope of the mountain as I tumbled with him.

He screamed as the terrifying heat enveloped us both. I
somehow remained on top of him. Fire licked at my boots.
Our faces so close, we brushed ears. He thrashed under me.
His raging gaze locked on Athena, who stood rooted in
place as if she held up the sky like a pillar on the Acropolis.
With a burning white hand he raised the barrel. My hand
scrabbled against his.

The hammer fell. Athena's eyes met mine through the silky
red fire. "I could only bring you to the edge of hell," she
said. She toppled into the hungry flames. Her white buffalo
skin curled.

Hands gripped my shirt, heaving me off Coyote's heaving
body. Eithne picked me up as if I weighed as much as a
newborn child. She sped into the snow-covered pine trees,
under branches, over logs. Coyote's hungry howl rang in
our ears.

Night closed its inky grip on the mountains. Alan weighed
on my shoulders. The branches whipped my face and arms.

I felt my god-strength waning, and my heart with it. I
tripped, and we sprawled under a great pine. Alan tumbled
off me. The dead needles stung my palms, wrapped
themselves in my hair. I cast my hands at the air and
howled. It echoed endlessly on the mountains. I clawed at
the ground with impotent fingers. Coyote would find us
again before we could reunite with Mother! Before I could
have my revenge!

My vision cleared, and I saw Alan staring at me. I saw a gleam under his eyes. His hand rose to his head, then down to his navel. "What are you doing?"

It was a halfhearted, automatic gesture. He failed halfway. "Sending Athena's soul to God," he murmured.

"What for?" Comprehension dawned. "You think…that's absurd."

"You saw what happened."

"Nothing like that could harm her."

"You saw her." His voice trembled. "You saw her burning."

I caught him by the scruff of his neck. My breath felt hot. "How is that possible?"

I saw confusion in his eyes, but also unbearable certainty. "She was human."

"You're lying." I cast him away from me. He hit the pine solidly, grunting.

"Why would I lie?"

I had felt it. The shifting in the order of the gods. It couldn't be real. It had to be a trick, an illusion. "How do you know?"

Alan crossed his arms, defending against the cold. "She could not cross the fire."

I saw Mother's crackling buffalo skin. I saw her grimace of pain as the heat of the flames touched her. Was that acrid smell from the boiling fire, or the thunderstick?

It was no illusion. My nose would not lie.

I collapsed, moaning like a wounded rabbit. Why was she so enamored of humans that she would die for one?

I didn't see him move until his hands touched my shoulders. I buried my face in his chest. I heard his silent prayer, felt the tremors of his own grief. Had he ever experienced such loss? Had he ever loved someone so much, he thought they would live forever? The stars stared down at me accusingly. I protested to the whirling winds, to the steep earth. What could I have done?

"I think she thought it might happen."

"What do you know about it?" I kneaded the back of his shirt. My eye-rain flowed. When at last he tried to pull away, I still clung to him. At last he removed my hands. "Why did she save you?"

He looked away. "Because of my gift."

"She knew what it was?"

"It is what any man has."

"Why didn't you use it to save her?"

"I do not know how to use it."

The trees mourned Mother's passing. Save for the chill mountain wind, the world had silenced after the fall of a great pillar. An owl hooted. As much as I wanted to blame him, I knew Mother wouldn't approve.

I tried to read Eithne's expressions. Her grief had been surprisingly short. That put me on guard. Eithne had always been unstable, but now I had no idea what she would do.

Her face was blank. With rage? Mourning? "Coyote will chase us."

"Surely he burned to death in those flames."

"Those are his flames. They will not impair him for long."

What could I do to escape this wretched beast? I thought I had been safe. But even the gods could fall. My power was world changing. What kind of power did man have, to make the gods kneel before him? What could make one such as Athena…

I had not wanted anyone to die for me. I had just wanted to evangelize the Indians. And even that had been snatched away from me.

The gods were once human.

Perhaps…perhaps, if the gods had once been human, a greater power had bestowed it on them.

"Where are we?"

"We're at the top of the pass."

"How long would it take to make to Denver from here?"

"If I carried you, we could make better time."

"Is that all right with you?"

She curled into a ball and closed her eyes. "That is a silly question. I do what I have to do."

What she had to do. All the talk of power, of purpose, of the claim Coyote had on me, froze me in ice. The leaves stirred beneath the snow. Trapped. "What of New York?"

"Why would you want to go there?"

I looked to the devil's thumb. "I know how we can at last be rid of Coyote."

I saw the gleam of fire in Eithne's eyes, and her shiver. My own hands were white as old bones. I thought back to the first night we had traveled together. Even gods could chill, it seemed. And the night was very cold. I tried to remember what month it was. I guessed it to be mid-December. The dead of winter.

I moved next to her. Tonight would be a very cold night, and we would both need all the warmth we could get.

Chapter 11

Eithne carried me on her back when I could walk no longer, and I walked with Kuruk's cane when she could carry me no longer. It had not been the most comfortable means of travel, but Eithne did not seem to register her own fatigue. I had to climb off her back myself. Whenever I looked at her, she was looking back. The snow silenced the world, and the trials of coming down the pass once more ate at our strength and reserve. My knee twinged whenever I moved it. I could walk, but not well, and not for long. Athena's face floated next to Chief Left-Hand's in my nightmares. I often woke Eithne up.

We had both been run ragged by the two-day trek. Even Eithne's feet were bloody by the time we left the mountains. Mine looked like slabs of raw beef.

At last, when we rose above the last hill and gazed on Denver, I sank to my knees. Eithne stared beyond it, to whatever visions of the past had entranced her.

Denver. And after that, home. How would I face my parents?

I looked over at Eithne. The white snow grayed her eyes, dulled her flaming hair. "I suppose this is where we part."

To my surprise, she shook her head. "I need to make sure you are safe from Coyote. I will travel home with you."

In the distance I saw a cloud of steam traveling down the mountain. "I think I will take the train back." Then I remembered. "I have no money."

"Is money needed to ride a train?"

"Yes, and I lost it at…Sand Creek."

From her clothing she produced a small sack. "Would this do?"

She handed it to me. I tipped the sack into my hand, and small yellow nuggets rolled out. "Gold!" I exclaimed. "Where did you find this?"

She bit her lip, still staring into the plains. "Everything a goddess needs is given to her."

I strung the gold pouch about my hand. "I see. I will not ask further."

We walked into Denver. It was evening, but light enough for the train station to still be open. As we walked, passersby looked at us sympathetically. One or two even attempted to press a coin into my hands. When I made it to the train station—a small one, but neatly kept—people gazed in awe as I thumbed out a small gold nugget to pay for our tickets. We would ride the Continental railroad, and finally the smaller lines until we reached New York. I shoved the tickets in my pocket and took Eithne's hand. She let me drag her down the street to the same saloon we had stayed at months ago. I paid the keeper, who did not recognize us, and we went to our room.

"I recommend a bath," I said as I arranged my bed. "We will be on the train for several days."

Eithne nodded absently. She stared out the window. I continued. "After we bathe, we should buy some new clothing. The gold is more than enough to pay for nice things, and it is still evening."

She gave me a blank stare. I cast about for something else to tempt her with. "I saw a nice restaurant. We could go have some chicken."

Something sparked in her lifeless eyes. "With butter?"

"If you wish."

She got up. "Where is the bath?"

I bought myself and Eithne comfortable traveling clothes. I decided on a suit and fedora, and Eithne, a green dress with a brown petticoat, and a white umbrella.

"What is this?" she said when I attempted to give it to her.

"An umbrella."

"What does it do?"

I opened it. She jumped back, eyeing it warily. "It keeps the sun and rain off you. It is common for women to have these."

She took it, hooking it over her wrist like I showed her, twirling it experimentally.

I looked at her, really looked, for the first time. She had become a goddess of a different kind. A great lady. She had even combed her hair. Delicate, like a flower. Was this really the same girl who had beaten an entire bar full of drunkards senseless?

We left the tailor, and strolled down the street toward the restaurant I had mentioned. I hooked my arm with hers. She cocked her head at my gesture.

"It's proper for an escort to link arms with his lady."

Her eyes fell to the ground. "I see." She actually seemed embarrassed.

We arrived at the restaurant. It was well-kept, catering to the more gentlemanly of Denver's population. The tables had been polished, and the floor well-swept. Not overly crowded, and far from the more rowdy, disreputable saloons.

We sat in a well-lit corner. I ordered for us both, and we sat in comfortable silence. Eithne pretended not to be interested, but her gaze kept darting about. The tightening in my chest eased when I noticed her curiosity in her surroundings. Right now, I just wanted normalcy. No gods, no giant coyotes, no burning books. Just calm, and a nice dinner.

The waiter brought out a salad. Eithne almost grabbed at it with her hands, then pulled back and studied how I ate it. I held up the salad fork. "Use the longest one for the greens."

She obeyed. She ate slowly to cover her clumsiness with the unfamiliar utensil.

Our waiter brought out the chicken. Eithne's eyes widened in expectation, and I saw visions of her sweeping it off the plate and eating it whole. Instead, she folded her hands on her lap while I carved the portions. I watched her struggle with the knife. "Hold it like this."

I showed her how to hold it. "Cut small portions. It is not seemly to wolf down big bites." She mimicked my actions, and took a small bite of chicken. Her eyes rolled with pleasure.

The soft conversation which had permeated the room stopped suddenly. I looked up from my instruction. A dusty, bedraggled man had just sat down at a table. One of the patrons said, "He does not have the decency to take off his coat?" Another whispered, "They should throw him out."

I ignored him. He could come here if he could pay. We had just finished the chicken when I noticed a wave of silence in the patrons' chatter coming our way. I looked up again to see the same man walking our way. His black beard quivered, and he looked somewhat out of sorts. I assumed he would go past us to the bathroom. Instead, he stopped at our table. "Can I help you, sir?" I said politely.

"I think ye cain." He reached into his jacket. I found myself staring into the black hole of a gun barrel. The other patrons could not see the gun. I raised my eyebrows. "I assume you want my gold."

He grew unsure, not expecting my reaction. "That, and the pretty wench."

Eithne bristled. I moved to touch her hand, but the man's gun wobbled. "Calm down," I said. Let's not be hasty."

"I want 'em. Now."

"You do not want to cause a scene."

He blinked. "I'll be waiting outside. Don't think to escape, I got a man around back." He jammed his gun back into his jacket, then went to the restroom. I made eye contact with Eithne and shook my head in mock disappointment. She lifted her lips grimly. "It seems you have grown a backbone."

"It gets almost boring after the fifth time." As I said this, my racing heart steadied. "Is there another man?"

"No. He lied."

Shortly after, we paid and left. "That man is desperate," I told Eithne. "He will not give up easily."

"I can deal with him." She bared her teeth. Predatory…almost hungry.

He jumped us in an alley. His gun wandered as he tried to stare us down. "Gold, woman, now!" he said, his voice taking a shrill edge. He seemed more frightened than we were.

I raised both of my hands, then slowly reached for the pouch of gold in my jacket pocket—the outer pocket, so he could see I did not possess a gun.

"Toss et to me."

I threw it underhand. It landed at his feet. "I would have been willing to give you money," I said. "If you had asked."

When he reached down to pick it up, Eithne attacked, sweeping the gun out of his hand and poking him in the stomach with the umbrella. He collapsed, groaning. I started forward, but Eithne flung herself on top of the man. Abandoning the umbrella, she lashed out with her clawlike fingernails. "Eithne—"

The man gave a muffled yelp. Blood welled between her fingers. "Eithne—"

She doubled back her fist, and punched him soundly in the face. She punched him again, snarling. He struggled, but she pinned him with her legs and dress folds.

The man screamed in agony. I reached for one of Eithne's flailing hands and missed. "Eithne, stop! You will kill him!"

The man's screams grew tenuous. I hurled myself bodily on Eithne in an attempt to restrain her, wrestling her arms to her sides and pried her heaving body off her unfortunate victim. I glanced at his face, then away. She had reduced it to pulp.

I held Eithne's head in a viselike grip. She struggled, but I forced her to look at me. She snarled in my face, but I saw the tears running down her cheeks. Her teeth bared, her snarl turned into a sob. She beat my chest ineffectually, her strength spent. She quivered under my fingertips.

"Come on." I looked to where the man had been. Only the gold pouch was left. I stuffed it back inside my pocket.

I helped Eithne to her feet, and she leaned heavily on me the rest of the way back. I murmured whatever I thought would keep her calm. When we made it to our room, I left her to herself to get into bed, while I stared at the fire in the common room.

I tried to make sense of what Eithne had done. Part of me was appalled at her actions. In the past I might have attempted to lecture her. But part of me, the part that had witnessed the massacre at Sand Creek, reveled in her actions. I had wanted to join in, to pound my own angst into the dust.

I stared at my hands. Once they had been soft, but for calluses on the first two fingers of my right hand. Now they had spread. I was no longer innocent. And neither was Eithne.

I returned upstairs to go to bed.

I woke up sometime in the middle of the night. Silence spread its inky tendrils through the clear, bright air.

Eithne perched on the windowsill. The moon reflected in her eyes, the stars on her soft, bare flesh. The wind rustled her long mane of hair. With barely a sound, she dropped out the window.

I did not wait for her in the morning. I packed our things and went to the train station alone, half expecting her to appear beside me as I boarded the train. I even handed both tickets to the conductor. He looked at me strangely.

"Sorry," I said. "My mistake."

I pushed past him into my carriage and found the cabin. As the train chugged forward, I looked out the window, searching among the milling crowd. I kept searching even after Denver had become a speck in the distance.

I expected her to appear, and half-wished she would not. If she were gone, I could pretend everything was normal.

I closed my eyes and tried to imagine myself as I had been. Tried to imagine that same person coming home. The vision dissolved in a cloud of smoke. I had half-convinced myself that she would stay. But after what had happened, I should have known better.

I refused contact with the other passengers. At lunch and dinner, I stayed in my cabin. I could not face another chicken. Finally I decided to go to bed early.

I awoke from a dream about Elizabeth, trying to hold on to the bittersweet memory a little longer. The pounding at my door knocked it out, however. Grumbling, wondering who would disturb me so early in the morning, I stumped to the door and opened it, in nothing but my drawers.

"What is it?" I growled.

The person growled right back. I blinked, cleared my eyes. It was Eithne. Wearing…

"Come inside, and please, cover yourself!" I whispered hoarsely. I had forgotten that she had left naked. I turned and tossed a blanket at her. I heard her pick it up and slip into the room, closing the door behind her.

We had no more privacy than we had out in the wilderness, so I was used to her dressing up while I stood with my back to her. I pointed to her things and waited. Finally, she said, "I'm finished."

I turned. She had donned her traveling clothes. "Where have you been?" I exploded, before I could stop myself. She regarded me with a mixture of irritation and…a smile.

"What are you smiling about?"

Her smile twitched. "You."

"Indeed. Where were you? I thought you had…"

Her grin vanished. "What? That I had left again?"

I averted my eyes.

"You still don't trust me?"

"I do not know what you will do from one moment to the next."

Her eyes narrowed. "If you must know, I was searching for signs of Coyote."

"Why did you forsake your clothes?"

"I didn't want to ruin them. And they would've been a hindrance, anyway."

She struck at all of my weaknesses, especially those I was vulnerable to as a man. My treacherous imagination stirred. It had done so throughout the time I had spent with her, but never this strongly. One would think I had better things to think about when a god nipped at my coattails.

I moved without thought, gripping her shoulders. She met my eyes. I smelled the soft fragrance of lupine, felt her tense beneath my hands. Her lips parted. Her hands met my bare chest, and her eyes searched my face.

The dream, my memory of Elizabeth, came between us. "Do not do that to me again," I whispered. I released my hold on her. "You must be tired. The beds are small, but comfortable."

Weariness washed over me. I collapsed into my own bed.

My heart thrummed like a hummingbird's. The moment Alan had touched me, the only thought that penetrated my sudden, unreasoning panic was how furry his chest felt. I pulled my paws back.

I gathered myself enough to say, "Sleep well, priest." He grumbled and turned over. I flopped onto my bed. I had taken the trouble to clothe myself fully, so I wasn't going to bother stripping again.

I woke in the middle of the day. The iron horse still bumped along the iron path, leading to more iron paths which would take us to Alan's New York. Alan had described New York to me, once. A big place, with many buildings and many people in them. It seemed ridiculous that so many could live in one place. Were they stacked on one another like sleeping gophers?

I wandered out of the mobile den. The small tunnel-hallways allowed only one person at a time to move about them. Following the aroma of food, I slithered through to the next den. I sniffed traces of chicken seasoned with pepper, but to my disappointment, they served soup.

Alan was at a table with his back to me. Other people talked, but a few looked at him curiously. I stared at him for a few moments, noting his slumped shoulders. He looked broken, defeated. A plucked eagle. It was no wonder the other passengers looked at him that way.

I slipped behind him. I reached out to touch his shoulder, but thought better of it and moved to sit across from him. He looked up. "Oh. It's you."

"Naturally."

He continued to play with his cross. "Do you believe in God, Eithne?"

Before now, I would have laughed at his question. But he needed to lick his wounds. Maybe I understood the nature of this wound. I answered, in a low voice so others wouldn't hear, "What are you hunting, priest?"

He looked up at me quizzically. "What do you mean?"

"You were set loose on wilderness you don't know. You can't see whether it would be best to hunt, dig a den, or give yourself up as prey. You don't know if a corn stalk would grow on top of a mountain."

"Can they?"

"No."

He considered my question for awhile. "You're saying that what matters right now is what I do, not what I believe?"

"Yes." I nibbled on a finger.

He steepled his fingers. "Why don't you believe in God?"

"I am one. I have not seen Jesus, therefore I don't believe in him."

"What god blessed me with this power, then?"

"You're a priest, so I assumed some other god had blessed you. I know the gods. Jesus isn't among them."

"Athena seemed to believe in a being higher than herself."

"She always had strange ideas."

"Indeed."

"I haven't seen him, so I don't believe in him. What about you, priest? You see, but do you believe?"

His face became blank. I knew I had made him angry. "Stop calling me that."

"Calling you what?"

"Priest."

"What else would I call you?"

He stood. "I am going back to the cabin. You should eat."

He left. I pondered his questions for awhile. Perplexed by his sudden exit, I didn't immediately register the new smells emanating from behind me, toward the front of the cart. When I did, my lip curled, and my insides curdled.

Coyote had come to me. He would feel my jaws on his jugular.

Coyote laid a hand on my shoulder. "I think you're right, you know. She always had strange ideas."

I whirled out of my seat. I met yellow eyes. But the face was wrong. He hid behind Alan's face, a snake imitating a fallen branch. "When did you…how did you-!"

"You didn't see the band of humans waiting over the next rise, did you?"

From his waist he pulled out a thunderstick. He shot it into the roof. The mustard stench of fear washed over me as the other passengers panicked. One woman screamed, another fainted.

"Listen up!" Coyote barked. "This is a robbery. Will you kindly hand over your valuables to this young lady?" He nodded toward me.

I growled. He shifted the end of his barrel. "Do not make this hard."

"You want to shoot me?" I laughed. "Go ahead. We both know what will happen."

"Maybe," he said, and fired.

I flashed my teeth. "See? I—"

Someone gasped. I looked down. Blood spread across my dress. "Y-you…"

I sank to my knees. My mouth moved, but no words came out. My eyes widened to push back the creeping darkness. A cold fire spread through me.

Coyote leaned down. He whispered, "What strength do you think you have?"

His teeth closed on my ear.

Was God mad? Or did he simply not exist? Reality itself was mad. How was I to decide what to believe, when the sky turned upside-down? Eithne said I should act, but what power did a man have? What secret strengths hid in these weak limbs?

I noticed a strange movement outside the window. A man, leaping from a horse, onto the train.

A loud pop resounded above the clattering train wheels. I turned back to look into the dining carriage. Scruffy ruffians pointed pistols at men, women, children. A robbery. How many dangerous situations could I get into? If I could just get to Eithne…

Someone put his hand on her shoulder. She leaped to her feet, then recoiled in confusion. His gun pointed at her midriff. She bared her teeth.

The gunpowder's smoke trailed thinly between them. Eithne fell, with a spirit's grace, to her knees.

"No!" My hand rattled the carriage door. "Not for me!"

The man who shot her turned. I met myself. My lying self. He had yellow eyes. Coyote…but why did he wear my face?

He pointed. One of his –or mine?— accomplices shouldered past him, his intent spelled out in the grip on his revolver. I turned and raced for the next carriage, but stopped when I saw another man shouldering his way through terrified innocents.

Of course. The shootout in Denver, the wanted poster. He had done it. He had been that blue-eyed boy's death. As I would be the cause of Eithne's...

I careened into a compartment. I had to find a way to her. But how? Fight those men? They would beat me senseless. There had to be something here, perhaps I could use as a weapon...

My hands scrabbled across the cushions, in the carriage racks, over the latch to the window. The train raced along a circuitous path on one side of a great rocky gorge. It swallowed the snow in its dark depths.

I opened the window. The sheer dropoff of the gorge flashed beneath me. The wind's bite had the edge of a wolf's teeth. I had lost my marbles. Only one thought pounded through my veins. It would not be Eithne. Anyone but her.

I clambered out the window, making use of my strong hands and back. I might walk with a limp, but I could still crawl. I gripped the roof tenuously, a rush of fear driving me onward. I was mad. But this whole journey was mad. I was god-touched, insane!

I hooked one arm on the roof, then my other. My fingers dug into the grooves in the wood planking. The curve prevented me from surmounting it with my legs inside the train. I would have to swing out of the window briefly.

I glanced inside. Loki's lackey had made it to my door. Out of the corners of my vision, the startled faces of the other passengers watched me with awe. I kicked out of the window, holding on for dear life.

I heaved upward. The hand holding Kuruk's cane slipped. I glimpsed the gorge's sickening maw.

The beak of the cane caught the edge. I grimaced. A leaf whipped past the wooden eagle's eyes. This was a debt I could never repay.

First my left leg, then my crippled right. The rushing wind and bumping track threatened to throw me off. I gritted my teeth. "Stupid leg, do not fail me now!"

I crawled toward the dining carriage, gaining purchase from the small ridges in the roof, trying not to think about the bonecrushing fall, the locomotive wheels catching me, turning me into jelly…

One inch forward. Over the whistling wind, I heard my pursuer yell something. When I turned back, he had gone inside. Presumably to cut me off. I had not thought of that.

I tried to stand, steadying myself on the central rib.

"Oy! Priest!"

My doppelgänger stood on the dining car, waving his hat like a bull rider. "Did you need some fresh air or summat?"

"When Eithne finds you, she will kill you!" I shouted back.

"Really? She didn't look worthy of that last time I saw her."

A cold lump formed in my gut, fears roiling with fears. "You will answer for that!" Niwot's hand reached out to me as the yellow eyes bored through my soul.

"I showed her a mercy."

"Mercy?"

"Yes, boy. So she would not become like me." He swept his arms wide. "Now, why don't you let me take that burden off your hands?"

"Never!"

He squinted. "I thought you might say that!" He waved wildly down the track. "Look over there!"

I looked down the track. A bridge spanned a gulf some hundred feet wide. My bowels clenched.

"You see that, priest? I rigged that bridge to blow." A slender hand had appeared on the edge behind him. The lump in my gut traveled to my throat. Everyone on this train was about five minutes away from a horrible death.

The hand became two. Loki continued. "If you don't give me your power, my partners will blow the bridge."

"God," I croaked. "Dear God, why have you forsaken me?"

Bright red streaks of hair flailed above the carriage lip.

"You don't want that on your conscience in the afterlife, eh, priest?" Loki cackled. "Oh, that's right. You're no priest!" He danced a jig, waving about acrobatically. "Decide quickly!"

I watched him dance, oblivious to the deaths he would cause. Oblivious to the pain and suffering he had inflicted on the Arapaho. Oblivious to the enraged, mourning goddess behind him. His sick, disgusting frivolity. I howled my defiance at him through the whirling wind. "You want it then? Come and claim it!"

Loki grinned. His teeth shot out from his gums, nose from face, morphing into muzzle. His clothes exploded off him as fur rippled across his skin.

Coyote leaped at me. I closed my eyes, preparing for my death.

The gargantuan thump of his massive body reverberated through the carriage. I felt his hot breath, heard the snapping teeth. My eyes popped open, and I staggered back. Eithne, with superhuman effort, had latched herself onto his back. He snapped at his encumbrance, but Eithne gripped his ear, wrenching it. He yelped. With the last of her waning strength, Eithne threw Coyote. He sailed onto the next carriage, collapsing like a ragged doll.

Eithne's momentum carried her along. She slid down the roof, caught herself, dangling by one hand.

I was too far away. I would have to let go, rely on my balance to get to her.

I crouched low. I slid down, my hands scrabbling for purchase. I snagged a handhold, my crippled foot dangling into open space. I retracted it, and reached for Eithne. "Hold on!"

Her face was pale. Her gray eyes, bone-white. A bloodstain on her front rippled in the razored wind. I tried to focus on her hand instead of her life trickling off the edge of the carriage roof.

Her grip weakened. I lunged forward with my last inches, and gripped her wrist. I said the first thing that came to mind. "Eithne! You still haven't had my mother's chicken!"

She grimaced, growled. Her other hand flailed, then latched onto mine. I pulled, and she scrambled up. She held onto my shoulders as I dragged us both to the top of the carriage.

Her mouth next to my ear, she coughed. "You lied to me."

"Yes. I lied to you. I lied to the world. I was no priest. I had no god."

"Why?"

I saw no harm in telling her. Not when we were about to die. "My personal fantasy. My dearest wish. To bring God to the godless." I wrapped my arm around her. "Instead I found you."

An explosion reverberated through the mountainside.

"Coyote," Eithne breathed. "He burned the bridge."

I did not look. Instead, my eyes were drawn to the cross about Eithne's neck. My cross, which she had been forced to bear. I watched it flutter in the wind, took it in my free palm, then turned my gaze to Eithne's pallid forehead resting on my chest. "Eithne…Do you believe in justice?"

Her voice was faint, a dying breeze in a howling gale. Her answer flew away. With the last of her waning life, she locked her eyes with mine.

I closed my eyes. The cross dug into my palm. How to tell her? How could I convey my gratitude, my thanks, my love? My faith in her?

What did she love most?

I cupped her cheek in my hand. Those gray eyes had stared beyond me long before she met death's river. I would repay my debts. I would choose the straight and narrow path. No more running. No more worshipping of false idols.

Her lupine scent was fading. "If we live," I said to her unhearing ears, "You will hate me forever." For this was not a lie, not the one which had brought me here, but the brutal truth.

I met her cold lips with mine.

Her eyelashes brushed the frozen droplets on my nose. Her breath melted them. She grimaced as she forced herself to her feet. The blood which had seeped from her ghastly wound had stopped. Her skin, deathly cold and white before, radiated heat and life. The very air pulsed around her. She snarled wordlessly.

Tongues of flame leaped from her hands, her feet, swirled about her in torrents, like the time on the pass. Water and earth surged from the sides of the tracks, snaked about her in ecstatic coils. The dead leaves of autumn, like fluttering souls, danced in the tornado of nature. Enraptured by the sight, I could only tremble.

The mass of elements enveloped her, then flew outward, scattered to the four winds. In its place, a great being loomed over me. The roiling wind ruffled through white-gold fur.

I reached out and touched my cross, still about her neck. "Who but God could have created someone like you?"

Her great ears perked. Those magnificent gray eyes, filled with knowledge and the weight of hundreds of years, closed. Her tails danced in the wind, the essence of fire, the kindling flame of being. The world around her became a slow dance, snowflakes twirling, wind puffing, caressing.

An organic rumble beneath the jounce of the train tracks raced toward the bridge. I turned from Eithne and beheld...

At first I could not make sense of what I was seeing. The bridge seemed to reassemble itself. As we crossed it, I saw ears of corn, low-hung squash, and a flash of tiny pods dangling, freezing in the December air.

She had grown a new bridge. She had bent scraps of metal and wood to her will with beans.

Eithne bounded toward me. She swept me up in her teeth, tossed me like a newborn kit. I felt no fear. Only warmth.

I landed on her back, where I clung to her soft fur. She turned to face Coyote.

Coyote limped to his feet. The boundless hatred radiated from his eyes; his lashing tail rocked the carriage beneath him.

Eithne bunched, bracing herself for an attack. A tongue of flame burst into being between her ears. Coyote shrank back, his ears laid back. Eithne leaped backward, floating gracefully onto the next carriage.

Coyote frothed at the mouth, creeping closer. He swayed back and forth. Eithne mirrored his movements. They feinted at each other, nipping at ears and muzzles, their smallest movements upsetting the train's delicate balance on the tracks.

Eithne reared, punching Coyote with her massive paw. Coyote sprang forward, teeth flashing, but Eithne locked her jaws in his neck. He yelped and twisted, but Eithne held fast. He screamed in pain. It echoed horribly off the mountains, ringing in my ears. I smelled singed hair. Between Eithne's jaws, Coyote's flesh smoldered.

With great poise, Eithne growled and twisted, catapulting Coyote onto another carriage, denting the roof. He rose, spluttering. Eithne jumped, and I held on for dear life. Coyote snapped at Eithne, but she pressed him into the roof.

Her paw slipped. Coyote lunged. For me. I tried to ward him off. My hand pressed on his forehead.

It smoked blackly where I touched him. He howled. Black smoke oozed, then billowed, from underneath his fur. He shrank. When the smoke cleared, he had returned to the thin and wasted body of Brand.

Eithne shoved him off the carriage roof. He caught the edge with his fingertips. Eithne bunched underneath me again.

"Wait!" I laid a hand on her neck.

I scrambled off her back. I sensed Eithne's incredulity. But I could not watch him die if I could help it. "Eithne, help me."

Her words whispered in the fullness of the roaring wind. *According to your own law, he must die.*

"Hang the law!"

I staggered. She snagged my collar with my teeth. I reached out to Loki. Coyote. Brand.

"You killed my cousin," I shouted over the clattering tracks. "You killed Athena. You betrayed your people. I don't think you deserve to live."

Loki looked up at me with hopeless eyes. Another bridge over a grand gorge would open below us soon. I brushed his fingertips. "But it isn't up to me."

Confusion distorted his face. I saw Larson in his eyes. And Niwot's regret. I saw myself.

"Would you consign yourself to hell?" My hand scrabbled on the back of his. "I can give you new purpose! Bury the hatchet!"

The gorge opened beneath us, the maw of Dis waiting to swallow its prize. I saw what he would do, a moment too late.

His grip slackened. A flurry of snow swallowed his wasted frame. His eyes, staring at me, all the way down. Falling, like a parched autumn leaf, buried in snow. Soulless.

Eithne panted, tremors running up and down her length. Her paws gave way beneath her.

I took her giant head in my hands. White smoky light enveloped her. Her god-form evaporated, leaving behind a trembling, pale, naked girl.

I wrapped my coat around her. "Come on."

She met my eyes. Wordlessly, she encircled her arms about my shoulders. She kissed me on the cheek.

Chapter 12

Remarkably, no one had seen the battle between Eithne and Loki. They had obviously heard it, and felt it. Stories raced wildly as to the explanations, but I put about the tale that the would-be robbers had set up a rockslide to scare everyone. The passengers had been busy dealing with Loki's hooligans. When a war veteran had brained one with his walking stick, and a young tailor had tackled and subdued another, they at last had time to notice the dents in the ceiling. In the confusion I had been able to carry her into our quarters. Quite the adventure, climbing back into the carriage while half-frozen, and corkscrewing breezes threatening to carry us away.

Her traveling clothes were nothing but rags on the wind now, so she dressed in her formal attire. Some recognized her as the one who had been shot. She responded to their queries with, "A miracle. A simple miracle." She gave me a fake, shy smile. I acquired the attention of every passenger.

"God watches over us all," I said.

Eithne enjoyed the attention. She mingled gracefully with the other passengers, using the social skills I had taught her. She sometimes appeared contrived, but only I noticed. And only I noticed how her hands trembled, and her troubled glances in my direction.

"We should throw these two into a gulch." The war veteran stroked his moustaches, peering gravely at the two hooligans they had subdued and tied to the seats. They cringed. "We should. But I do not think the good priest would take too kindly to that notion."

"Indeed," I said. I chose not to say I was not officially a priest. It did not matter to them.

"We will hand them over to the proper authorities at the next stop," I said. "As much as I sympathize with throwing them down a cliff, the matter of life and death should not be turned over to we who are prejudiced by circumstance."

"Well said." The young tailor nodded.

The veteran pulled out two cigars from his voluminous jacket. One passenger, whom I presumed to be his wife, rolled her eyes. "A smoke, to your good health, young lady." He proffered one to Eithne, who took it graciously. She held it up to her nose, and sneezed.

"God bless you," I said.

Eithne cocked her head at me. "Indeed," she said, mimicking me. She glanced at her cigar, then back at me.

"Does the lady not smoke?" The veteran pawed through his jacket for matches.

"She has never smoked before," I said.

He grinned, lighting a match. He lit his cigar with aplomb. Eithne stared in fascination. "He lights it on fire…on purpose?" She sniffed the smoke, first with delicate inhale. Her lips twitched. "I would like to try this."

I would have liked to stay. But I needed to think. I used the crowd's growing liking of Eithne to my advantage and slipped out of the dining carriage to my quarters. She would be all right.

I watched Alan go, even as I fumbled to light the smoke-stick with the fire-stick. I wanted to follow. I wanted to glory in Coyote's defeat with him, and mourn Mother's fate. To ask him what that kiss had meant…why he held such power to heal or condemn a god with it.

I puffed on the smoke-stick. My eyes watered. I coughed, and the man with fur on his face chuckled. "Refrain from inhaling so deeply," he said. "Not for your first time."

My nose felt like it had been cleaned out with burning chaff. "How can you do this to yourself?" I asked.

I spent the rest of my time with them. They were very boisterous, relieved that no one had died, reveling in what they perceived as a miracle from their God. I reveled with them, but one question stuck like a burr.

Smoking soon led to a vile-smelling drink. Strangely addictive, that drink. It made me feel all hot and free.

Later that evening, I stumbled into the cabin. "Alan, come on!" I grasped at his shirt. Missed. I giggled. "There's thiss stuff you have to try. I think they called it bark juice, but it's like no tree I've tasted…"

He caught my flailing arm. "You are drunk."

"Iss that what it'sh called?" My mouth felt all cottony. I stuck my tongue out.

"Yes, and it is a sin."

I peered at him, swaying one way, then the other. "Kind of like lying. Isn't that one too?" I swayed forward. He caught me. I felt his biceps, laid my forehead on his chest.

"You do not have to tell me that."

I craned my head back to look at him. "Didn't stop you though."

My emotions were a confused jumble. Woozy, happy. But something with claws, not the strange happy-water, was dragging a precious treasure of mine down a dark hole.

I let Alan drag me to my bed. I flopped over like a dead fish. "Why did you?"

"Why did I what?"

"Spare Coyote."

He didn't answer for a long time. "For the same reason Athena died for me."

His words kindled cinders. "And why did she…"

"For the same reason you helped me."

"Sstop playing games and get to the point."

"Very well." He sighed, rubbing his temple. "I have a purpose. It took me a long time to see what it was. I thought I was supposed to evangelize the Indians. Instead, it seems I am supposed to evangelize the gods."

I giggled. I felt hot, suddenly. I plucked at my dress. "That is…silly."

"And why is that?"

The shoulder of my dress slipped. "You should know better by now."

"Athena seemed to think my power was meant for something." He didn't notice me undressing. Even in my fuzzy state, I could see when he had the predator's eye. He had focused in on his new goal, like he had focused on the Arapaho. It left me strangely cold. It was intolerable to hear him yapping like this.

"She…had a lot of strange ideas."

His eyes blazed. "What I do not understand, is how you can deny everything she said! She clearly meant for us to find meaning outside ourselves, the straight and narrow…"

My head lolled. With a grace borne of alcohol, I slipped out of the dress, off the bed, and into his arms in a single movement. He caught me.

I licked his neck. He twitched. I sensed his growing desire. My fingers dug into his back. He raised my face to his own.

The fires stirred within me. If I had been my normal self, I would have been wary. But the burning spread, and with it, my aching need. I touched my cheek to his, whispering in his ear. "I am a god. Do you need anything else?"

He stiffened. His hands fell.

His push was firm, gentle, and distant. I fell back onto my bed. The fire drained from me, leaving ashes.

"What will it take to make you see?" He dared to look sympathetic, as if I needed pity. If he had been anyone else…

My paws opened and closed. They felt numb. My gaze dropped to my thinly clothed front. Instead of wanting to bite him, I wanted to hide. To crawl somewhere dark and curl up until I starved.

"Why?" I asked again. I felt very tired. My eyes drooped. "I don't understand."

How could he make me feel this way? What was wrong with me? What would I have to do to…to…

"Why what?" I heard his words from far away. Something warm and…callused, touched my forehead. "You are drunk. Get some sleep. You will regret the morning."

He was right. I did feel horrible. And I didn't remember most of what I said—or did—for a long time. I avoided him as best I could. When I did see him, I averted my eyes.

The other passengers looked at me with an intimacy bordering on reverence. I found it unsettling. They looked at me the same way Alan looked at me. I found myself on edge for no apparent reason, jumping when someone touched me on the shoulder, flinching when a hem of a skirt or cuff brushed me. They expected nothing of me. Yet I felt a responsibility to them because of what I had done.

I gradually withdrew from the company of the other passengers, curling into a window seat in the lounging carriage. Coyote's last expression floated through the glass with the sun's dwindling rays. That fear, the hopelessness, when Alan had snatched away his most precious possession.

I lifted my hand, stared at it. Alan's words from this morning came back to me. Evangelizing the gods. Did Alan promise Coyote's fate? What good could come of losing the very thing that made you who you were?

Alan sat down in front of me. Absorbed in my own thoughts, I hadn't noticed him. I began to stand, but he caught my arm. "Please."

The look he gave me sent sympathetic tremors through my fingers. "What do you want?" I said. He averted his eyes. I hadn't meant to say it that way.

"I am sorry for last night."

He was apologizing? "I...I am, too."

To my surprise, he waved it aside. All of my assumptions about his feelings whirled away in a cloud of dandelion seeds. Perhaps that vile drink had made me imagine his arms crushing me to him, the heat on his skin. "Do not apologize for that. You were drunk."

He had taken it completely in stride. And I had just made a fool of myself. My jaw stiffened. "Have you come to your senses then?"

"What?"

"Your ideas are nonsense."

"I was apologizing for the way I reacted. Not for my beliefs."

"Then why bother?"

His brow furrowed. I expected a retort. Instead, he said, "I wish to help you, Eithne."

"Is that how you see me?" I said through clenched teeth.

To my befuddlement, he appeared confused. "What are you on about?"

"You pity me. You think I've lost my way. You want to…to evangelize me." I couldn't help the fear creep into my voice.

"Of course I do. Athena wanted it, too-"

"Stop talking!" I growled. "Stop talking about her. Who are you to decide who I am? To decide the fate of gods?"

I swept out of my seat. He caught my arm again. He held me in a velvet prison. "Everything has a reason, Eithne. I have this gift for a reason. But I will not take your freedom from you. Only you can decide to walk this path."

I turned, faced him. My paw clasped his. "Promise?"

His other paw covered mine. "I promise."

He embraced me. I had held myself stiffly, but his touch melted me. I trembled.

"You know," he said, "I heard chicken is on the menu again for tonight's dinner."

I dragged him out of the carriage.

Our time on the iron horse had ended. What had taken Alan a moon-cycle's time to travel, took us a quarter of the time. It took a little longer, because humans, the curious beings they are, wanted to know what had happened with the attempted robbery. We had to dispose of the two rascals as well.

A week after Loki perished in the gorge, I saw the sun dawning on the largest human dwelling place I had ever seen. A city, with thousands –tens of thousands?— of people. We stopped at a platform. I saw them, bustling about like bees, everywhere droning, tipping their hats to each other, laughing, and shivering in the snowfall.

Alan took my hand. "Are you ready?"

His face had become white as limestone. Looking at the packs of people, I felt mine do the same. "No."

I had faced many things, but the crowd was the most daunting. I couldn't keep track of them. In the plains, I saw miles. Here, I saw feet, inches. Alan pulled me off the iron horse, helping me down the step when I stumbled in my dress. He led me into the crowd, parting the sea with his cane. Men, women, children, all of them pressed against me. Alan urged me on. My hand nearly slipped from his, and I clung to it fiercely. "Why are you in such a hurry?"

"It has been almost a year," he said, breathless. "I have been away for far too long!"

He waved at a horse-drawn carriage. It stopped for him. He paid the driver, then sat in the carriage. I sat beside him. I hugged myself. Such a busy place. The sights, the smells, all of it pressed down on me, an enormous boulder rolling on my chest.

I glanced at Alan. "You're like a kit that has just learned to swim. You're still afraid of the water."

He averted his eyes. "I do not know what to expect."

"You're not lying. But you're not telling the whole truth, either. What is it?"

He stared out the window. Pretending not to hear me. Very well. If he didn't want to answer just then, I wouldn't press him this time. I would give him that courtesy in apology for our previous quarrel.

The carriage clattered down the cobbled street. Taller buildings gave way to smaller dens. "You don't have to tell me. If you don't want to."

"It is not that. I am just not certain…"

"About?"

"About how they will react to you." Still not telling the whole truth.

"You taught me well. I know how to behave."

"You are forced. You haven't the breeding a woman in my society normally enjoys. I do not know how my family will take to you."

I had guessed this already. "You're still not telling me something."

He took a deep breath. It came out ragged, shaky. "I do not know what to say to them. About my travels. About how I missed them. How I want to apologize to them for abandoning them. About…Angus…"

His shoulders shook. I stroked the back of his head. He still hadn't told me everything, but it would be wrong to wring more out of him.

The carriage stopped at the outskirts of the city. I clambered out, fighting with my ridiculous dress. Alan offered his paw. I used it to preserve what little grace I had left.

The carriage clopped away. No doubt the horse was glad to see me go. A grand living-den loomed over us. I marveled at how many windows it had, and the creeping vines festooning the trees and sneaking onto the walls. A gate and low wall hemmed in the grounds. In the distance, horses frolicked in the wide field, but unlike the horses roaming the plains, a fence blocked them in. "Alan, is this truly where you live?"

He didn't answer. He saw a scene different from me. Perhaps the walls were bigger for him, the trees more threatening. Or perhaps he looked at it as a long-conquered frontier. Dangerous in its familiarity.

I touched his paw. He took mine. We started along the stone path. As we walked, Alan's movements became storklike. At last, halfway up the path, he stopped. He murmured something.

"What?"

"Take me away."

"Take you where?"

"Away from here."

I let go of his hand and planted myself in front of him. "Where would you go?"

"Back to Colorado. Anywhere!"

I crossed my arms. "What if I refused?"

Taken aback, he floundered. "I will...I—"

"I don't understand what it is you're afraid of. You've faced down a god."

"It is not that simple."

"Neither was Coyote."

He glared at me. Then the fire left his eyes. His shoulders straightened. "Very well. If I can commit to that...I can find a way to commit to this."

I took his paw again. This time, I felt a hesitation in his grasp. As if my touch burned him. "Come on. The anticipation is worse. Like diving into cold water."

"Yes." He straightened his collar. "Yes, you are right."

We made it to the grand double doors. They smelled of a different land, of foreign rain and soil. I eyed their dark paneling. "Your family is rich."

"Yes. Did I not mention that to you?"

"No, you didn't."

He raised his hand to knock. Before knuckles touched wood, the door opened. An old man in fine clothing appeared. He was very old, for a human, but he held himself firm and straight, like a great tree. "How may I help you?"

"Shane. Do you recognize me?"

He blinked. "I beg your pardon, but I do not think we have..." He squinted. Then his eyes widened. "Master Cormac? Is that you? It has been almost a year. We thought...but we hoped..." His craggy face cracked into a smile. "It is good to see you! Your mother will be overjoyed! Come in! Oh, but I am forgetting my manners. Who is the young lady?"

He had tears in his eyes, but he refused to shed them. Alan, struggling with his own emotions, said, "She is a friend, someone I met on my travels."

"I see. Any friend of Master Cormac is welcome in this house."

I wobbled my curtsy. My face reddened. "I feel welcome already."

In truth, I felt like the maw of a mountain lion was closing around my neck. But this Shane seemed kind. The den was beautiful.

I glanced at Alan. He hadn't recovered. The first knock had not been the end of his struggle. I tried to pin the source of his vexing agitation. But he hadn't told me anything. He had many secrets.

The Shane man led us to a small room to the side of the grand staircase. I stared at that staircase.

"Do not stare so," Alan whispered. "You look like a country bumpkin."

I was about to tell him where he could put his bumpkin, but the Shane interrupted me. "Shall I prepare some tea?"

"Yes, thank you." Alan's eyes fell. "Where is my mother?"

"She is out at the moment."

"I see. And...how is Elizabeth?"

"I am sure she will be eager to see you again," Shane said. His words sounded like spider's webs.

"What about my father?"

Shane's hands shook. "I am sorry, Master Cormac. He…passed away. Some two months ago."

Stricken, Alan hid his face with one hand. When he recovered himself enough to speak, he pursed his lips and said, "I see. How stands the will?"

"The family has been…I suppose it would be best to let your mother tell you the details."

"They are fighting."

"Yes, Master Cormac. Your Southern relatives have come. Your father left everything to you, but since you left—"

"The war went ill for them, I hear. Now, their money is worthless. And they do not want their trip to go to waste." Alan straightened, his eye-rain unshed. "I suppose there will be no opportunity for me to escape this time."

Shane nodded, his bow spilling out his respect. "Welcome home, Master Cormac. You were sorely missed."

"Thank you, Shane. How about that tea?"

We sat in a small waiting room. Alan stared out the window, absorbed in his troubles.

I had seen grief before. At Mother's death, I had felt it for the first time, keen, sharp. But seeing him, at the news of his father's death, made me ashamed. I had been selfish. Mourning her loss, I had taken Alan's compassion for granted. My station as a goddess had come before my concern over what he felt. Seeing him here, staring out the window, refusing to let the eye-rain flow…

"I…I'm sorry."

Alan shifted. "For what?"

"I don't know. Everything, I suppose."

He shook his head. "I should be thanking you."

I touched his paw, which lay on the small table in between us. He patted mine, then stroked the stubble on his chin. "I had been running from my life here, my responsibility, in search of a hopeless dream. You made me stand fast, even when it seemed the world crumbled about me."

In the silence that followed, Alan's eye-rain broke at last. He hunched in on himself. I cast about for a solution, my eyes darting about as if the trees or the field could solve it.

I rose from my chair and knelt at his feet. Such a man, to make me kneel before him. I pressed my forehead to his, took his hands in mine. His tears flowed unchecked. I licked one from his cheek. He flinched, but I persisted. This was the only way I could express my sympathy. He seemed to realize that and let me lick drop after salty drop.

"You should stop. We would not want anyone getting the wrong idea."

What did he mean by that?

A voice like claws on gravel interrupted us. "What would you be trying to hide?"

Alan flinched and rose, leaving me on the floor. "Mother."

Gray-black frizzed hair exploded in all directions from a head in the shape and color of a ruby crabapple. The woman's teeth clenched and her brown eyes blazed like wildfire. Her paws moved restlessly at her sides. "After what you did, it as a wonder for you to see me at all. If you had done this as a boy, I would have treated you to the rod, and more. And to bring back this slip of a girl? I thought I taught you better."

I studied her face. Though she growled, and her gray hair flamed, she kneaded her green umbrella as if holding back a pounce. She didn't hold it back for long. She wrapped her arms around her son's neck. "You fool! Do you have any idea how worried I was? Fretting almost a year, imagining you captured by bandits or butchered by Indians!"

My lip lifted at her mention of Indians. Alan mumbled, but he returned the hug fiercely. "I missed you as well." He let go of her. "Mum, this is Eithne."

She eyed me up and down as if she faced a rival over a choice morsel. "Pleased to make your acquaintance. I am Ciara Cormac. I hope you will forgive my earlier remark. I spoke out of turn."

"The pleasure is mine." I curtsied. "But I am in some confusion over which remark you refer to, that of me or of the Indians."

The Cormac woman pursed her lips. "To what are you referring—"

"Ah, mother," Alan said, "She used to live with the Indians. I believe you offended her at the mention of them butchering me."

"I forgive your remark," I growled, though I smiled sweetly. Alan's lying was improving.

The woman's eyes turned to granite, turning her smile to a grimace of challenge. "So you lived among the Indians? Is that how you met my son?"

I couldn't help snorting at the memory. Alan glared at me, tempting me to wrinkle my nose at him. "Not precisely. The Dineh captured him and I happened to pass by."

"Dineh?"

"An Indian tribe, mother."

"My goodness! Tell me everything."

Alan and I looked at each other. I knew what I would say. Alan did as well, for he started before I could utter another word. He apparently thought mentioning my godhood would be a mistake. I only sought to put the woman in her place after all, even if she was Alan's mother. "Eithne has lived on the frontier for much of her life, so she knew the signs of a raid. She saw me captured, and rescued me that night. After that, she offered to be my translator. We have been traveling together ever since."

"Why did you accompany my son home, my dear?"

"I wanted to meet the family. I have heard glowing recommendations of your chicken."

"And you, Alan? Why did you finally decide to come home after all these long months? Why is your fool of a cousin not tracking mud through the halls?"

I saw in his mother's face, a mixture of emotions. Disapproval, mostly. But in Alan, I saw everything. He choked on his words. "Angus is…he…" His shoulders slumped. I leaned my shoulder into him, hopefully without this Ciara-woman noticing.

His back straightened. He gave a tremulous smile. "He married. He is living among the Indians now as far as I could find out. I never saw him in the West."

She gaped silently. She held a hand up to her mouth. Alan had said it with quiet grace. As if he really believed his cousin was alive and happy. I had thought him a bad liar, but even he could produce one when it was needed.

The Ciara-Cormac wrapped her son in another loving embrace. "There, there," she said, patting his head. "You were close to him, I know. I am sure he is happy." She pulled away to look at his face. "I am glad you are home."

"I was such a fool," he murmured.

"Yes, you were. But you are back. I shall save my telling off until after Christmas."

"Yes." He straightened. "I am back. I will do what I can to lead this family."

His mother eyed him up and down, as if Alan had transformed into a different man. A stranger. I shared her sentiment. Alan had changed, from a wandering milk-drinker to a strong, capable hunter.

"Some family members will protest your return."

"No doubt."

"Your father's plans can still be put into action." His mother glanced at me swiftly. I was puzzled. "Elizabeth still waits for you."

"You do not have to worry. I will do the right thing."

His mother laid an apologetic hand on his shoulder. "You have had a long journey. We can talk about this later, when you have had time to reacquaint yourself with normal life."

Alan nodded. "I think that would be a good idea."

When she had gone, he walked over to the room's wall of glass. A door opened out to the brightening day. The clouds slunk back from the sun's clawing rays.

I was reminded of the kit, Larson. How he had looked when the judge had sentenced him. Trapped. Stifled.

I was a goddess of growing things. Not discord, or strife…or love. I didn't understand his world of whistling steam and cracking thunderstick. But I did understand him.

I glided to his side, entwining my fingers with his. His hand remained limp. "You have been shouldered with many burdens."

He sighed. "I have always carried them. I tried to run, but they overcame me." He met my eyes. The eye-rain hadn't left them, but he refused to let it fall. "Why do these things happen, Eithne?"

I searched his eyes, his soul. I took his head in my hands, and pressed my lips against his forehead. Another blessing. I gave him the peace of the wind rolling through the corn and the slow creep of the vine. "Summer turns to fall," I said. "Fall turns to winter. Winter turns to spring. Everything has its time."

Chapter 13

"The family will wish to see you, Alan." Alan's mother bustled, her head held proudly, like a moose. She looked nothing like a moose. More like a stork. But I could imagine her bulling through the forest. "You were spared the company this morning. They were at the theatre last night, so they have been sleeping in."

"Of course, mother. I will see them."

"Be polite. They may have been with the secessionists, but they are still part of the family."

"Yes, mother."

We were in a small eating room, what Alan called a parlor. I found the concept of a parlor ridiculous, and I told Alan as much. He had smiled. I had growled. When he had asked why I had growled, I said, "Your smile means you're laughing at me on the inside."

He chuckled. "Verily."

His mother chattered like a woodpecker at him, telling him many things I didn't understand, which she called "business." I understood the need for nuzzling up to make an ally, but the complex nature of their nuzzling, and the reasons behind it, left me baffled. My mind whirled in their talk of companies and stocks and investments. It sounded intriguing, but when I asked if I could learn, they looked at me as if I had grown two heads. Alan told me later that women weren't allowed to learn such things.

"But she knows."

"My mother knows because she was at my father's side for so long."

"Why can't I learn by yours?"

He blinked. "What…what do you mean?"

"Why can't I learn from listening to the two of you?"

His breath caught. I wondered what could be wrong with him. "Women do not do business. But," he lifted a finger, "I see no harm in you listening."

The afternoon dragged on in a dry, boring fashion. I found myself pacing the innumerable halls restlessly. Seeing no one, I wondered if Alan's family were phantoms.

I rounded a corner and ran into a mane of red hair. The hair, clothed in a dull gray dress, tumbled into a heap on the floor. I remained standing, of course. Not even a moose could wind me.

"How dare you!" The hair growled. The small, freckled face of a young kit bloomed among red hair. She glared at me. "Can't you see where you're going?"

"Watch how you speak, youngling," I said.

"I shall speak however I please." She stood up. She was a foot shorter than me. I grinned. She pouted. "I'm as old as you!"

"I doubt that."

"Who are you? Are you a new maid?"

"No." I eyed her up and down. "Are you?"

"I'm the daughter of Dylan Cormac, and I will not be treated so!"

"I do not care who you are, youngling."

She drew herself up. All this did was magnify her mouselike size. Her hair bushed out, destroying any chance she had at dignity. "I will speak to mother about this."

I waved my hand airily. The kit's face flamed. She raised her hand. My grin widened. "Go ahead. Hit me."

"Bridget?" A woman wide as a buffalo interrupted our standoff. The kit flushed a pretty shade of red. "Mother."

I eyed the woman up and down like I had her kit. Her jowls drooped, and her eyelids quivered, making her look both half-asleep and sly. I sniffed. No smell of Coyote, or any other trickster, but a distinct if faint tang of that vile happy-drink. Any trickery was her own.

She returned my suspicious look. "I have not seen you here before," she murmured in a gravelly voice. "Perhaps you are a new maid? No…" She peered closer, frowning. "A distant relative? What is your name?"

"Eithne. I am neither maid nor relative. I am a g…a guest of Alan's."

"Alan?" she jumped, her whole body quivering with consternation. "He is here? Alive? Why…why did he not call on us?"

"We arrived only this morning."

Her eyes narrowed. I smoothed my neck hair down. I didn't like either of them, though the fiery kit was amusing and somewhat adorable. She would be fun to play with. "My name is Catherine. Perhaps he can formally introduce us," the woman said. "I am curious to see him and delighted to hear of his return." She smelled angry rather than delighted. She gestured imperiously to her kit. "Bridget, come along. It is almost lunch-time, anyway."

We turned down the hallways, passing woven pictures and stone carvings of people's heads. The heads were perplexing. Some Indians scalped their enemies, a recent practice I found distasteful. But what was the purpose of carving their likeness into stone?

I looked closer, reading the names, but they didn't enlighten me, either. Not until I came across one bearing the name "Cormac" did I understand.

I had fallen behind them. I ran down the hall to catch up.

"The relatives are awake," my mother said. We had heard the thump, and briefly the raised voice of my cousin Bridget. "At last. They have been frightfully unseemly since yesterday."

My heart sank. I had nine cousins, the oldest being Bridget after Angus. As much as I loved them, I detested being around them all at once. Individually they could be quite charming, but like fox and coyote, they were natural enemies. If I had remained in Colorado, and with Angus gone, Catherine's son Levi would have been the next likeliest to inherit the household, including all of the stock my father had purchased in the railroad.

I heard Aunt Catherine rouse the rest of her family. They tromped down the stairs, no doubt eager for lunch.

"Alan!" Bridget exclaimed. She raced into the parlor, flinging her arms around me. "Good to see you," I choked, staggering. "Please, be careful."

She tapped my cane. "What happened?"

I glanced at Eithne, who had glided in behind Aunt Catherine. "A long story," I said. "One you would not believe."

"Alan," Aunt Catherine said, "I am so glad to see you have returned safely home." She did not look all that glad, but then my aunt had always been sour. God knew, she had not much to be glad about, what with the war eliminating most of their wealth.

The rest of my cousins, all boys, squabbled among themselves. None of them had the distinct red hair Bridget possessed, nor the deep black I or my father wore. They were all either blonde or brown, with blue or green eyes. "We were so worried," Bridget gushed. "We thought Indian savages had got you!"

I glanced at Eithne again. Her glare at the back of my cousin's head spoke volumes. "Be careful what you say about the Indians," I whispered to her, nodding in Eithne's direction. Bridget scowled. "I don't like her."

"I think the welcome blessing of Alan's return calls for a celebration," Aunt Catherine said.

"The Christmas ball is only in a week. That would be the most appropriate time to celebrate the miracle of my son's return," my mother said. "Your friends have been lonesome for you." Elizabeth's blonde curls flashed in my head. Mother caught the look on my face. "Of course, it will also be a good opportunity to renew relations with business partners."

"What's a ball?"

Everyone stared at Eithne. She had let the fox into the henhouse, revealing her ignorance of civil customs. Now, my concern was hiding her godhood.

"I beg your pardon?" Catherine said.

I extricated myself from Bridget's grip. "Eithne was raised by Indians," I said. Only half a mile from the truth, but that was close enough. Bridget's eyes lit up. I groaned to myself. I had given her a means to needle Eithne forever more. It would likely result in Bridget flying over the moon.

"I had no idea," Aunt Catherine said. "She is so well spoken."

"I have taught her much in the time I have known her, but there are still gaps in her knowledge," I continued. "A ball is a party. We talk and dance. It is a form of play."

"I see." Eithne flushed.

I shivered at the thought of seeing Elizabeth again. What would she say to me?

If only father were here.

"Speaking of the Christmas ball," mother said, "I must speak with Shane about the decorations."

"The ball is nearly a week away, mother."

"And I have yet to decide on a theme!" She bustled out. Aunt Catherine and Bridget left as well, Bridget eyeing Eithne over her shoulder.

I turned to her. "We must find you a suitable dress for the occasion."

She narrowed her eyes in Aunt Catherine's direction. "I do not like them."

"They are my family. You will have to endure them for as long as you stay. At least you have a choice in the matter."

"How long should I stay?"

"You are welcome to stay as long as you please."

"Your mother seems to think otherwise."

"She has always been rather protective of me." I had lied again. I cursed my weak will. But I wanted her to stay. I could solve this. If I could survive long enough to return home, I could find a solution for this.

"Hmm." Eithne cocked her head at me. I knew she sensed I had not told the whole truth, but she did not press me. Her eyes wandered, and she drifted away to explore more of the house. I followed my mother.

Chapter 14

Knitting is ridiculous. While I was clever with my paws and had no trouble learning the knack, sitting for hours doing nothing but knitting bored me. The incessant birdlike chattering of gossiping women sharpened the boredom. I considered stabbing the furniture with the needles. Maybe I would chew on them as well.

"You made a mistake." The flaming kit, Bridget, studied my work critically. Someone had thought up the brilliant idea of putting us together, our apparent ages being the same. They actually thought me a kitling. How amusing. At first I had been indifferent to our pairing, but soon I wanted to poke her to death with my needles.

She continued in an exasperated voice. "It cannot be helped. Pull it out and start again."

I flung my work on the floor. "You do it. I'm sick of it." I stomped toward the door.

"Where are you going?"

"Outside," I snarled. It was too nice of a day to spend indoors with dull company.

"Savage," she muttered. "Try not to trip over yourself like you did learning those dances." She started to follow me out of the room. "I hope you don't plan on going to the ball tomorrow—"

I slammed the door in her face.

The bright sun warmed me, though winter's icy claws hadn't released their hold completely. I wandered into the back garden, to a small pond, curling up beside it in the sparkling snow.

I studied my paws. They had never been so white before. Always the sun had browned my skin, even in the infrequent times I walked in my human form.

"What am I doing here?" I whispered. "I don't know what I'm supposed to do."

For the first time in my endless life, nothing clamored for my attention. Humans managed the crops almost as well as any god. I could no longer hear the fox's chirrup. In these silent days, the only one that filled my life was...

Snow crunched behind me. A limping step. I dried my eyes.

Alan sat beside me. I wondered, as we sat in silence, if he had heard my whisper. He gazed into the mirrored pond, his blue eyes reflecting the glassy water. "It has been awhile since we have been together like this," he said.

It had been a long time. As he became more involved with his family, he drifted further away. The gentle breeze tousled his black hair. The look in his eyes made me ache. "Your cousin is a chattering squirrel," I said.

Alan nodded. "Neither of you seem to like each other very much."

"That is an understatement. I think she hates me." I continued, not fully realizing what I was saying. "I think all of them hate me. And I hate them. Not that I care, really..."

His shoulder stiffened, but I barely noticed. "This place is so stifling. It might be best if we—"

"You left?"

I looked up. I searched his eyes. I found anger, resignation, and a strange contentment. But what I wanted to see, I didn't find in his blue pools. "Don't worry." I laid my head on his shoulder. "I will keep you safe."

"What of your other duties?"

"I have no other duties. It is winter."

His suggestion hung in the air, though he didn't voice it. "Never," I replied.

"The world has changed, Eithne."

"No one needs me anymore, you mean," I said bitterly.

Alan contemplated his knees. "I need you," he whispered.

I studied him again. "I can't tell if you are lying."

"What about you, Eithne? What do you need?"

How could I answer? What would he say if I told him that until I met him, I hadn't needed anything at all? I would have gladly suffered and gone mad like Coyote before I had met him. But to get him was to give up everything.

I would live with him for forty years, at best. A blink in my timeless existence, and we would be gone. Could I face that kind of death with him? Could I face life without him?

We lived in separate worlds, obscured by a thin veil. We could touch through it, but we could never pierce it. But Mother hadn't remained with me on my side of it. And Alan could pierce that veil.

"You told me that everything has its time," he said.

I shivered. Something had changed in his touch; I felt it when he put his arm around me. A warmth that had coursed through him when we had stood together in the field of lupine. The gentle brush of his skin as he had cleaned the dirt from me at the healing springs. I wondered again if he remembered those moments, the searing ache, that bond between us tugging at each other's hearts like two wolves on a bone. "I know," I said. "But I'm not ready yet. Soon, perhaps."

My thoughts drifted back to the quarrel with the kit, Bridget. "Your family is not very forgiving."

"What makes you think that?"

I slid a lock of hair behind my ear. "I thought you saw how your mother looked at me when we first met. What did I do to her? Your aunt is slant-eyed as well. She's hiding secrets."

"Well, we all have secrets, do we not? Aunt Catherine has lived a hard life these past few years."

"Alan!" His mother's voice pierced the morning air. "We have a ball to prepare for. I need you!"

He stood, shaking of the clinging snow. "I must go." He departed, leaving me to paw the ground in frustration. I did not see him until the night of the ball.

I think humans invented corsets for torture. Perhaps that was because the kit helped me into it.

"You look like you are about to faint." Alan took my arm as I staggered into the foyer. "Are you well?"

"I can't breathe," I whispered. "Women dance in this?"

Alan had bought me another dress. I was starting to think he viewed me as some kind of plaything. It was a deep green, with sage trimmings. It highlighted my red hair, and turned my eyes a brilliant emerald.

I cursed the corset. "Eithne," Alan said with a faint smile, "Please refrain from using that language when the guests arrive."

I would have growled, but I didn't have the breath for it. Why had I gone along with this? Whose idea had it been, anyway?

Alan's family had lined up by the door, ready to welcome the first guests. The kit wore a columbine-blue dress. It made her look sickly. Her fat mother's red one made her look like diseased steak.

"Ah, here they are." The Ciara Cormac sounded short of breath, though she wasn't wearing a corset.

The first guests filed in like a stately rainbow. Dressed in numerous colors, the women glided in, escorted by sober-faced men. Some of them seemed oddly matched. One girl, a blonde no older than Alan, had been escorted in by what I first took to be the god of crows.

The girl curtsied to Alan with a grace even I found beautiful. She addressed him without being introduced. My eyes narrowed. She knew him. Three separate men had to introduce her to him in the past in order for them to talk freely. A silly rule. They exchanged pleasantries, but I sensed a deeper communication. The girl's face reddened, and she excused herself and glided away.

Over a hundred guests mingled with each other. I became separated from Alan, but I hardly noticed because I was too busy watching him. Many expressed surprise and relief at Alan's reappearance. He greeted each guest warmly, but I saw his hands trembling, his eyes darting. I wondered at the cause of his ruffling, for he had been looking forward to the ball.

With a twitch, I remembered I was supposed to be at his side. As his guest, it was the only way I could be introduced, and I didn't want to embarrass myself any more than I had done already.

I slid through the simpering, cunningly polite guests, and hooked my arm into Alan's. "I wondered when you would stop gawking and remember what I taught you," he said, patting my hand distractedly.

"I wasn't gawking," I hissed. "I was curious."

"Who is this fine young lady, Alan?"

It was the crow, stalking up to us. He bowed regally. He spoke with precision, pronouncing each word as if speaking with glass teeth.

"A friend I made on my travels," Alan said. "Eithne, this is Mr. Dawson."

"Pleased to meet you." I curtsied, wobbling slightly. I could force the weather to my will, but I still couldn't master the odd footing these people demanded as courtesy.

"My daughter, Elizabeth," the crow said, nodding to the blonde girl who had spoken so freely with Alan. "I'm sure she'll be delighted to meet you." He looked me over with raised eyebrows and icy blue eyes. I cocked my head, staring back, challenging him like I sometimes did with carrion birds.

Elizabeth glided toward us with stately grace. She had looked golden from afar, but up close she glowed. Her long blonde hair seemed to radiate its own light. Her smile revealed perfect teeth. Her eyes, wide and innocent and as blue as a mountain bluebird's, held Alan's in a grip stronger than a wolf's bite. It felt wrong to look at them.

Finally Alan remembered to introduce me. "A friend of yours?" Elizabeth turned her blue eyes to me when the introductions were complete. "You must have so many stories to tell, coming from the West!"

I grunted noncommittally. Alan dug his elbow into my side. "I have several," I said. "The first time I saw Alan, I was—"

"The music is starting," Alan interrupted, defeating my revenge. "It is time for the Grand March."

The chatter around us masked our next conversation. He led me away. "What were you about to say?" He was white with anger.

Startled, and angry myself, I said, "Stop watching me like a mother hawk." I grinned. "Should I tell her what really happened?"

"Stop being so unpredictable! Especially now!"

"But I like being unpredictable." The look on his face made me relent. "Don't worry. I won't tell them what I really am."

He was fighting himself on the inside again. "No…I know. I trust you."

After the Grand March came the spirited Virginia Reel. The guests split into packs of twelve, six men and six women. Elizabeth and her father joined our pack. After the first reel, the room spun like a dandelion seed on the wind, and I rode that seed high. Alan relaxed as the dances drained his strength. His whirlings cast off a heady euphoria, and I found myself muddled by it like smoke on a hot summer's day. The whirling tempest of bodies continued with another dance, a folk dance which called my god powers to flood the place, though not as clearly as the Rain Dance. The rigid and suffocating military two-step followed.

"We have such spirited guests!" The Ciara Cormac said after the dance had ended.

"Of course! We made the Rebs see the elephant!" one guest boomed. A cheer went up from most of the crowd, though Bridget glowered. What did seeing an elephant have to do with anything? Alan had never explained these phrases, though he had mentioned something about a war. Yes…the war the white-skinned fought over the dark-skinned. Rebs…rebels. Hmph.

"As you all no doubt know by now," Alan's mother continued, "my son has returned from the frontier and his inspection of the train service safe and well!"

Inspection of the iron horses? What was the woman blithering on about? I glanced at Alan, but he stared straight ahead at his mother. Why was she lying?

A furtive movement caught my hunter's eye, and a peculiar scent wafted through the stink of sweat from overheated dancers. It came from the direction of a table, where cups of what I hoped was bark juice alleviated the thirst of panting guests.

Alan had been waylaid by the crow-man to talk more of the iron horses. I slipped through the still-distracted crowd and sniffed at one of the cups. Tangy, spicy. Not the scent I was looking for.

My nose high in the air, I followed the scent out of the dance den and into the den where they prepared chicken and other delectables. I peeked around the corner and saw a flash of red. The strange smell rolled over me in waves, along with a trickster's rot. Alan's aunt stood alone in the center of the room.

My hackles rose. I slowed my breath and slunk behind a shelf. A feat of unimaginable dexterity in my ridiculous, restricting dress. From between two pans, I watched the woman.

More bark juice, four glasses on a platter, tempted fate balancing on the edge of the table. She wiped her hands on the front of her dress. From the folds in her clothing she pulled out a twinkling glass vial. She fiddled with the stopper.

That was the scent. The Trickster's rotten mustard smell coiled and reared.

Should I pounce? Or should I wait? Who was she deceiving?

She tipped her hand and sent two violently pungent drops into two cups. I held my nose. My eyes widened. I knew that smell. Fear's chill bite and rage's crackling flame-lick surged in my belly.

Elizabeth was intoxicatingly close to me. Even when I turned my head, the scent on her hair feathered through the air to paralyze me.

We stood silently together as my mother spoke, and I took in not a word. Elizabeth's hand brushed mine. Her fingers closed about my shaking digits, then retracted, leaving behind a small, round, hard object. The ring I had given her.

I met her eyes. She looked down to my neck, where the cross she had given me should have been, taken by a wayward goddess. Eithne had not given it back.

I became aware of my surroundings as the crowd clapped. "Where did she go?"

"Who?" Confusion crossed Elizabeth's perfect features.

"Eithne. She disappeared." My intestines knotted.

"That red-haired girl?"

I scanned the crowd for her brilliant auburn crown. "Yes, the one I met in Colorado."

"I imagine she has gone off to sulk somewhere over her horrible dancing." Aunt Catherine appeared out of the milling crowd. Mother, red-faced, joined us as well.

"Mother, did you see Eithne?"

"No, dear. My, I was never as good at public speaking as Seamus was!"

Shane, our beloved butler, approached us with a platter. "Care to wet your throat, Mrs. Cormac?"

"Ah, Shane, you are punctual as ever." Mother clasped a glass gratefully.

"I would not mind a bit, either," Aunt Catherine said, taking a second off the platter.

Foiled by the trappings of society, I took the last two and gave one to Elizabeth. I hoped Eithne was behaving. "To the health of our great family," Catherine said.

We raised our glasses together.

A flash of red caught the corner of my eye. Flashing gray eyes and a billowing dress barreled through the four of us. All four glasses flew into the air, their contents cascading on our finery. "Eithne!" I spluttered. "What on earth—"

I blinked. She faced Catherine, her arms wide. Her hands were claws. Her tail, which only I could see, flashed, twitching, rod-straight. Her eyes burned crimson.

I reached for her. My fingers closed on empty air. She pounced on Catherine, who shrieked as Eithne's claws tore at her front. "Eithne! What are you doing? For God's sake, stop!"

The guests looked on in horror as I grasped for Eithne. Catherine's shriek turned into a crazed roar. Eithne had touched her…a god had touched her.

"Get off her!" I encircled Eithne's waist and heaved her bodily into the air. She thrashed, her elbow hitting me on the head. She snarled wordlessly as I carried her out into the back yard. The crowd of guests watched us go, silent, unmoving, startled deer in a meadow.

"This ought to cool you down." I dumped her face-first into the snow. She leaped up and stumbled over herself toward the door. I shoved her back. She howled and went for it again. We butted heads as I dug my feet in and struggled against her. I smelled the rage's iron tang on her. Every movement she made was frenzied.

She panted. I gained ground. "Desist, Eithne!" She panted harder, pushing with all her might against me, but we were deadlocked in our embrace. "Eithne, you are very close to being thrown out. I may be able to intercede, but my mother will be out for your blood after what you did to Aunt Catherine. We both know how this might end. Please, quell your wrath."

At last, she found words. "She nearly poisoned you! You and that blue-eyed bird!"

"What? Elizabeth?" I started, dropping her hands. Her declaration replaced my anger with bewilderment. "How do you know?"

I eyed her warily. She made no move for the door. "I smelled it."

"I cannot say that to my mother."

"Then tell them the truth. Tell them what I am."

"Then what? They would sooner stone you than believe you."

"I can take it."

"I…I cannot." I could not see her brought so low. But now, how could she stay now?

Her hands clenched, but the stars washed out the expression in her eyes. The cold snow had washed away the crimson. Her tail vanished, and her claws softened into hands. "What am I, Alan? What purpose is left in me?"

"I do not understand…"

"Coyote! Why do you think he became what he was? His reason for being, his guardianship, had been stripped away from him!"

A cloud passed over us. Eithne's gray eyes shone with their own light. "Are you saying I killed him?"

"No. He killed himself. You saw that yourself." The cloud passed over us. I wished it had stayed. The stars stared down at me with twinkling accusation. I felt hollow, ashamed.

"What am I to you? Am I your tame god? How can I live here, when I have seen the things humans do to each other?"

"You could not go back to the Indians, then?"

"I am no longer their god. I cannot help them against the horrors of other humans."

"I…" She was right. Forgive me, Niwot. Catherine. God forgive us all. "Is that how you perceive us?"

Of course it was. It was how I saw us as well. My jaw ached from the clenching, but the pain in my soul was…I felt heavy.

Was this how all the gods saw us? Had even Athena looked on us with contempt? Had Coyote been driven mad by our actions? "We are horrible. Depraved. We are hopeless. All of it deserves the deepest punishment." I reached out to her with pleading hands. She would see this as a betrayal. "But that is all. I am not trying to sugar it. Sometimes, we do horrible things to each other. I have forgiven them."

She recoiled, snarling, trapped. "How can you say such a thing so easily? Forgive? When these humans—"

"Athena told me something. She said you were not just the goddess of corn, beans and squash. She said your passion was for America itself. You wanted to safeguard its soul. You are more than a goddess of food."

The shining moon froze her in silvery marble, caught in the light of Apollo's gaze.

"You are running away just as I was. You are goddess over my people just as much as the Indians."

"No, I am not! I am *your* god! From the moment I saved you, I became yours!" The marble shattered. "I will take you away. I will—"

"Force me to go against my will?" I shook my head. "No, Eithne. I know enough of your kind now to know that is not allowed."

She took my wrist. I laid my hand on hers and pried off her fingers one by one. "I belong here. I can no longer run."

"With you, I don't have to run."

My eyes sank to the ground. "I can never be with you. Not if we are to be truly free of Coyote." I released her hand. It dangled limply at her side. "That is what humans are. We cannot help it. Even you cannot change the nature of the human soul. Coyote had a claim on me. I forsook my family's needs, my duty, to go into the wild. It was a boy's dream, a lie to myself. The only way to make reparations was to come back."

"But we defeated him!"

"No. I defeated him when I decided to board that train." The icy wind kicked the snow. It was cold. Leaves perished in the cold. "This is my decision. I…cannot be fair to you. I cannot give you what you wish. It is not just. But it is right. My purpose is here, with my family, and it is also to the gods."

"I don't belong here, Alan. Everything here is told through a veil of lies. Your kin. Your love."

Had Athena foreseen this? Had her plan been this all along? What good could come of this?

My eyes burned, and my trembling lips wished to speak her name one last time. Her hands clenched at her sides. How out of place she looked here, in that dress. I should never have clothed her. But if I had not, I never would have known her. "Falling in love with you was like falling in love with the wind. I can touch you, but I cannot grasp you. You blow through my hands."

"So you're saying you don't love me. Is that it?"

"No. I do. I never lied about that. But unless you relinquish your powers, nothing right will come of this. Even what you did to Catherine is paltry compared to this."

She raised her chin stoically in the face of my choked declaration. "What about that woman, Elizabeth. Eh? Do you think I'm stupid? I know you, Alan. You promised to her first. The bond I forged when I rescued you is void! It has to be, according to your own rules!"

I looked down at the ring on my left hand. "Yes."

She traced her cheek where the small scar the musket ball had given her still lingered. "Let me go, Alan."

The smell of lupine grew faint. "Loki was right. It was a dream. We tell lies to ourselves." The snow sank its frigid teeth into my hands. "I do not want you to leave."

"I don't belong here. Your life is a prison to me. Mortal life itself is a prison. Out there, I can chase the chickens, and slink in my beloved cornfields. I can watch the land grow and change."

"But to be alone forever? To never know the love and companionship you deserve?"

"But you belong with me!" Eithne swayed like a great tree in a gale. She bit her lip. "What spell did you cast on me? To capture me, the free goddess? You lied to me all this time, and I can't even hate you for it!" The dead leaves whispered from their wintry graves. "I should have left you to die. I should never have interfered."

"Then strike me down now."

"What?"

"Kill me. If you think I never should have lived, then correct your mistake."

She raised her hand. Her fingernails shimmered in the moonlight. Her starlit eyes, running like an autumn rain, then stilling into clear pools. Her gaze flicked to the moon. Her hand fell to her side.

"When the last of the gods are gone, and you are left alone, what will you do?"

"Would I find love here?"

I looked away from her. It felt wrong, to see her crying. "Not the love you seek. If I am to undo the damage I caused when I left, I must devote myself to my other commitments." I whispered into the darkness. "But I will always cherish you. You will always be welcome in my house."

She pressed something into my hands. "I see now what Mother meant." Her last words were a breeze, a breath, in the still air. "It was always yours. But I think you've earned it now."

She brushed past me. When I looked back, she was gone. The dress, tumbling in the wintry wind.

I did not know how long I lingered. The moments ambled past, stretching into years. I began to see with Eithne's eyes. Time itself was immaterial. For her, the few months she had known me was a blink in eternity. But because she would live forever, that blink would last an eternity.

I looped the cross around my neck. I shuffled back inside, to the warmth and light.

Later that evening, I knelt beside my bed to say the Lord's Prayer. "Our Father," I began, "Who art in Heaven, hallowed be thy name. Thy Kingdom come, thy will be done, on earth as it is in Heaven. Give us this day our daily bread..."

Bread. Wheat. Corn. The images swirled before my eyes. The memories of Eithne laughing in the cornfields would haunt me forever. Her roguish grin. Her halo of red hair. The feel of her soft, silky skin. The warm scent of lupine. Her whole body, radiating life itself, giving it to the land. She had not been wholly honest with me, either. She was no mere goddess of plants. She was the free goddess of summer, the deity over the New World.

My prayer changed. "God," I said into the dead quiet of my bedroom, "Is this Your will? Have I done the right thing?"

I might have heard an answer. But that could have been the winter's chill wind crackling the frozen glass of my window.

Epilogue

The woman walked down the street. Her green hood and cloak flapped in the thawing breeze. Her red hair, like tendrils of life, escaped the hood and warmed the air. People caught a flowery scent as she sped by. No one took a second glance at her, yet when their eyes moved past her, they felt as if they had just missed seeing something extraordinary.

She waited at the street corner for a taxi. An old Model-T rolled to a stop in front of her. "You're looking for a ride, miss?"

"I am." The woman pushed back her hood. A stray droplet of rain from the overcast sky hit her nose. She snorted the droplet away irritably.

The taxi driver raised his eyebrows. This woman could hardly be called a woman, no more than seventeen years old. Yet she held herself like a matron of an extended family, or a duchess. The taxi driver heaved himself out into the chilly air and opened the door for her.

She imperiously took a step forward, but missed the running board. She stumbled, cursing like a sailor. The cab driver, chuckling, held out a steadying hand. When the girl took it, he caught the ghost of a smile across her lips.

He smiled back, only half aware of what he was doing. When she had been safely seen into the automobile, he groped for the handle to the driver's door. He missed it, and the girl smiled for real this time.

"Where to, miss?" he said once safely inside.

"Do you know the Cormac estate?"

"I do."

They rolled down the street. The taxi driver kept looking back at his charge. Once, he almost ran over a dog. He swerved, apologizing furiously to his passenger. But she simply smiled, and stared out the window.

The rain started to drizzle. The girl held a hand out the window, catching the rain. She brought it in, sniffing it. Then she sighed.

It had a strange effect on the cab driver, watching her mood swing from amusement to melancholy. His tone was apprehensive as he tried to engage her in small talk. "Have you been to New York before, miss?"

Her eyes penetrated his in the rearview mirror. "Not for a long time."

"Are you visiting for pleasure or business?"

"A little of both."

"You're acquainted with the Cormac family then?"

She raised an eyebrow at him. "Are you Irish?"

He smiled. "Half. Father Cormac has done much for the Irish immigrants."

"I see." An awkward pause. "Father Cormac?"

The cabman looked at her strangely. "You're going to the Cormac residence, and you've never heard of him?"

"Alan is his first name, correct?"

"That be him." The cabman slipped into his Irish accent as he grew more comfortable. "He's been about forever, teaching and preaching. What sort of business d'you have with him?"

"He's an old friend. I haven't seen him in a very long time. I knew him before he became a Father, you see."

"Oh, he's not a real father. He's a lot like one, but he never became a priest. We call him Father, because he's like one to people like me ma."

"That sounds like him." Her smile was simultaneously quirky and sad. Like she had remembered an endearing trait of a long-lost lover.

Silence fell inside the cab again, and remained until they stopped. The driver got out and opened the door for her once more. "Thank you," she said, and she pressed a bill into his hand.

The driver wasn't listening. He looked as if something had struck him heavily on the side of his head. "How do you know Father Cormac from before...how old are you?"

She patted him on the cheek, slipping into a rolling Gaelic accent. "Don't trouble your head about such things, m'boy. Just know, the world isn't as simple as it seems."

She strode up the cobbled walkway, leaving the driver dumbfounded in the softly drizzling rain. Her footsteps made no noise. She glided, like a fox in grass. The rain soon cloaked her form.

She continued up the path, through the gate, and to the doors. She knocked at the double doors and stepped back. Her eyes moved to the overcast sky. They reflected the gray clouds. Her countenance, once full of life, seemed haggard. Her hair, which had radiated the last rays of the sun, now hung limply; what had been golden strands were now gray. "Perhaps even I am too old for this now," she murmured.

A maid with bushy red hair answered the door. "I'm here to see Father Cormac," she said to the maid.

"I'm sorry, miss, but he's very ill. He isn't supposed to have visitors—"

"All the more reason I should see him." She hesitated, finger twirling a lock of her auburn hair. The maid was surly. Just like her grandmother, likely. "I'm an old friend. Tell him Eithne has come to see him."

The maid looked her up and down, nonplussed. "I will ask Grannie Bridget." She disappeared into the mansion, leaving the guest in the rain. "Hmph. How rude," she said, shaking the accumulated water off her hood. "I suppose it isn't any surprise. She does look just like her."

Her ears perked as she heard raised voices inside. "I don't care!" an old woman's voice shouted. "You will leave the answering of the door to Simon! Now, go wash something!"

The door opened once more, and an ancient woman peered out at the uninvited guest. Her wispy hair, once a bushy red mane, had been pruned to a few white wisps. "You're not Eithne," she growled.

The girl smiled. "Bridget, I presume?" She put a foot in the door. "May I come in?"

Grannie Bridget gestured irritably. The girl hopped inside smartly and helped the old woman close the door. "You came out here for nothing," the old woman said bluntly as the girl shook the rain off her cloak. "No one is allowed to see him, doc's orders."

"I'm sorry, but I can't wait." She smiled, hoping to win her over with winsome charm.

The girl expected a sharp retort. Instead, Bridget met her with a strained silence. "You do look a lot like her," she muttered, half to herself. "I am sorry, child. He's dying."

The smile on the girl's face died a slow, painful death. "I suppose," she said in a soft whisper, "I should have expected that." She met the old woman's eyes. Despite her denial, she caught a gleam of recognition, even fear. As it should be. "Please. I must see him."

Bridget dithered, grumbled, then finally gestured upstairs. "He's upstairs in his room. I can't walk those stairs any more. You'll have to go up yourself."

"I know where he'll be."

"Hmph." She tottered into an adjacent room, dismissing Eithne with a trembling wave of the hand.

Eithne hopped up the stairs, balancing on each as she gazed about the old mansion. She paused to examine each old bust, each stern painting, and more recently, photographs, as she ambled down the hall.

An intriguing collection of objects caught her eye. Her eyes fell first on the Celtic cross and its intricate patterns. She traced them with one finger, following the lines down to the eagle's leaf, tied to it with a piece of leather. Her finger alighted softly on the dried lupine.

A small child's face peeked out from one room. She smiled at him, catching a whiff of…something. Like ripe blueberries. Her eyes widened. The child scampered back into the room. "A shy one," she said to herself.

She found the door to Alan's room. She rapped softly on the dry wood. There was no answer. If she had come this way, only to be too late…

"Elizabeth? Is that you?"

With relief and trepidation, Eithne pushed the door open. The room hadn't changed much since she had first seen it sixty years ago. Newer coverings, but old furnishings. Dust motes swirled from the rug when her feet pressed on it. And lying on the bed, a man just as old, just as withered as the lupine. Kuruk's old wooden cane leaned against his bedside table.

His eyes rolled in his head. Finally they focused on her when she sat on his bed beside him. "My God," he said. "It is you." He sat up slowly, tremulously. "You have not aged a day."

"Love me or hate me," Eithne whispered, her face downcast, "I'm here." It was both familiar and unfamiliar. He had grown old and lived as long as anyone could hope. She had lived in stasis, preserved in a seventeen year old body. The creeping claws of time could never ravage her countenance.

She gestured to the door, where the little boy peered in at her. He disappeared again. "What is his name?"

"James. After the man Paul wrote the letter to in—"

"The New Testament. A fitting name. I like it."

"Are you ready to accept your fate then, Eithne? Are you ready to truly find your purpose?"

She looked everywhere but at the withered old man in the bed. She couldn't tell his mood from his voice, for it was a voice used to wielding authority. A stern, calm, deep voice, but papery thin, nearly dried out from death's breath. "I've found it. I've found my purpose."

Alan's brow furrowed. "Eithne, you know well that the time of the gods is over. It's time to give it up. Find something new."

"I have." She hesitated. "Your presence has not gone unnoticed. The gods fear you."

"I am old, and only a man. I do not have long. What do they have to fear?"

"Some are irrational, evil." A shadow descended over the room, a cold, familiar aura. It must have been a dog that yipped outside. Yes, only a dog. "Some won't stop until your whole family is dead."

"They think the gift can be passed on?"

"I smelled it on your grandson."

He closed his eyes. "I see. And what will be your role in this?"

"I wish to be the guardian over your family."

He nodded heavily. "I thought you might say that."

Eithne searched Alan's face. "What's wrong?"

"I do not want you to."

Eithne blinked in surprise. "You don't?" She cocked her head in that familiar gesture of curiosity. "Why not? Do you not fear for your family?"

Alan looked up to the ceiling. He stared up as if reading words painted there. "I prayed for you to find your own path."

"What other path is there? How can I stand by and watch this happen?"

"This is," he shook his finger, as he had likely done so often over his lifetime, "exactly why. You see me and only me. You wish to bind yourself to me out of some misguided impulse—"

"Do you wish to know what I did these sixty years?"

Alan started, causing a cough to rack his brittle frame. "You are the first person in a long time to interrupt me like that."

"Indeed."

He laid a hand on his chest and nestled himself more comfortably in his pillows. "Very well. What have you been doing these sixty years?"

It was Eithne's turn to look at the ceiling. Remembering all she had done, the long, hard journey, not in distance but in time, and the long days and nights piecing together the fragments of scattered signs that could barely be called evidence. Scents, a thousand years old, followed a path of legends and old folk tales, weaving between gods, men, and the flesh and bones of the earth. "I was looking for my past."

Alan blinked. Eithne took this as a sign that he was
listening.

"Mother found me in Ireland. So I started there. I looked
for every legend that may have had a tie. I heard of the
Tuatha de Danaan, a race of kings descended from gods,
and a village they had lived in. There was a spell over this
village so it would only appear every few hundred years.
Using those faint scents, I divined the location of this
village. There I waited for many years."

Eithne twirled a lock of hair around her finger. "The village
appeared to me. Time works differently in their boundaries.
Their grandfathers could remember before the Christians
came to Ireland. They had driven out a Christian convert, a
young woman. A dark voice told them to drive her out of
the village, to kill her before their way of life was changed.
They drove her to the woods, into a clearing. Up a hill. The
girl had been pierced with arrows."

"There a great light blinded them. When they could see, a
beautiful being stood next to the girl. 'Because you have
slain one who has been chosen,' it said, 'you and your
village are cursed to live as this girl shall live. Your
judgment on her will become your own. You will be cut off
as you have cut her off, your glory diminished.'"

"I dreamed about it many times during our travels, not
realizing it was memory. I had been chosen for a task on
that hill. A purpose. A power to fill it."

"So," Alan said slowly. Eithne could see the moistness in
his eyes. "You were a Christian all along."

Eithne's laugh was half merriment, half sorrow. "Not as such, no."

"Irony abounds." He stroked his chin, though his face was clean-shaven. "Do you believe now?"

Eithne thought about that question for awhile. "I think I always believed, really," she said carefully. "I'm just not on speaking terms with him at the moment. I doubt I ever will be."

"That is better than nothing." Alan closed his eyes sleepily. He fell back to his pillows. All the energy seemed to drain from him. "I see now, I think. So many gods come to me thinking they were only made for one purpose. But you came with a new one."

"There is more."

"More?"

"Yes. When did you take Mother's power?"

Alan's eyebrow rose halfheartedly. "I was wondering when you would notice that."

"Hmph." Eithne rolled her eyes. "She accepted what you were before I did. Accepted her inevitable end. And she accounted for Coyote's desire. Hiding it in you was foresighted. But it had side effects."

"Side effects? Do you spontaneously quote excerpts of Plato?"

"That wasn't all of her power, as you well know. She was also the goddess of justice. Specifically, just wars."

Alan's eyelids fluttered. "I see."

"Yes." Eithne's gaze strayed to the window. The clouds seemed lighter. "I will soon be the only god left in America. I have been its dominant god for a long time already."

"So, there is still work left?"

"Men will fight wars, just and unjust, for a long time to come. I am glad to have a hand in the process. Mother knew me well. She saw it in me."

They let silence fill the gap. There was no need to go into disasters long past mourning. But Eithne's hand flew to her face. It came away wet. "Do you hate me, Alan?"

With great effort, Eithne met Alan's eyes. "Hate?" Alan smiled. It contrasted sharply with his withered countenance, for this was the smile of a man who lived a full life. "How could I hate you?"

Eithne trembled. She laid her head on his chest, still familiar even when it was so withered. "I wanted to come back as soon as I left. I watched you from afar." She lifted her face from the drenched sheets. "What must you think of me?"

He laid a hand on her brow. "I think you needed the time," he said carefully. His hand rested on her cheek. "I thought about you all the time. I knew you would come back."

"I have. I am. But not for the reason you think. At least, not the whole reason. I did want to see you…before you…"

She lost control of herself. She buried her face in the blanket. "It isn't fair," she sobbed. "Why must you grow old? Why do you face death so calmly?"

Alan frowned. "What is life without the possibility of death? I thought you would know this best of all. It is part of the cycle. Life dies and gives way to new life. It is a sacrifice we all must make in the end." He took her head in his hands, stared into her deep gray pools. "It is the toll we give to the ferryman after we live lives of regret."

"You've said this before," Eithne said.

"The gods have visited me over the years. I say this to all of them."

Eithne touched his face with her fingertips. They communicated in a language deeper than speech. Deeper even than the language of the gods. Spirit to spirit. An intertwining of eternal fate, of a destiny far beyond either man or god. Chambers of the heart. Beating together. Forever apart.

"I wondered what it would have been like," Alan said sleepily, "if you had stayed. But I think you were right to leave. We come from different worlds. You hated my world. I misunderstood yours."

"I'm here now," Eithne said. She sighed. "We're together now."

"Yes." He breathed slowly, in, out. "They say a man dies alone."

"You aren't."

"No. I am not. I have Elizabeth waiting for me on the other side." His eyes fluttered open to meet hers again. "But how will you live?" His eyes shifted, and he tried to turn his head. "My diary." He gestured to the bedside table.

"What does it say?"

"Everything. But there is room in it for you."

"Sleep, Alan. You're tired." She closed them for him with gentle fingers.

He nodded, and sighed. He searched blindly for Eithne's hand. "When I wake up, you will be there?"

Eithne caught his hand and traced the back of it gently. Her hands were steady; her answer, steadier still, like the roots of a frozen tree. "I will. I promise."

The light dimmed. The sun set behind the curtain of gray. The night grew still, silent, black. Eithne held his hand, his companion into the beyond. She sat in silent vigil, watching the night, alert, watchful for the prowling scavengers. When his grip slackened, she kept her vigil. She accompanied him into death.

Light filtered in through the window. It was white and soft, like dandelion seeds. With it came the chirp of birds, the smell of eggs and bacon. Even then, she remained with him, faithful to him, as the warmth left his body.

Someone knocked at the door. Without waiting for an answer, the person stepped in. "Alan? Are you awake? If you're hungry, breakfast is ready to be sent up…" the maid halted. She gasped. "Oh, I…Alan…"

She ran from the room. Eithne registered her on the existence of a rat. She was too busy taking in her last sight of Alan's face.

Hours passed. Shouts from the floor below disturbed the late morning peace, like the crowing of the rooster. "This is as far as I go," she whispered. "You were the only prey I couldn't catch. Rest well."

She laid his hand beside him. She took up the cane, her fingers falling smoothly into the grooves Alan had made in it with his fingers over the long years. Her face composed, her bearing straight and unerring, she walked out into the hall, the cane tapping beside her. She made it down the hall to where the shouting made sense.

"—a forgery! What kind of man would keep it hidden from his own family?"

"I witnessed him sign it, madam. If this person doesn't come to read it, then it is yours, but until the period expires, you can't see it. It's right here in the will."

Bridget and a man in a neat suit argued at the front door. Eithne walked up to them, but neither seemed to notice. "Excuse me," she interjected. "What is the problem?"

Bridget looked daggers at Eithne. The man in the suit looked her up and down, as if he recognized her. "What is your name, girl?" he asked.

"I am Eithne. Eithne of White Buffalo Woman."

"This is Alan Cormac's last will and testament." The man shook out a rolled piece of paper. He handed it to Eithne without further explanation.

Eithne took the paper gingerly. She read it without expression. When she finished, she looked up at both of them, letting no emotion escape. "It seems I have some work to do," she said.

"What is it?" Bridget pressed. "What did it say?"

"Alan has left all of his possessions to me."

Dumbstruck, the old woman stared at her, then at the lawyer. "There must be some kind of mistake," she twittered. "A mistake. He can't have meant you."

"There is no doubt, madam," the lawyer said. "She fits the description and she gave the correct name. And, he told me to give this to you as well." He pulled out a sealed envelope. Eithne took it and opened it. The paper was titled, *Birth Certificate*.

"I see," she said. "Well, he has certainly made everything easier."

She walked past the two of them without another word into the warm sunlight. The cold breeze caught her hair, sent it flying in all directions. "You believed in me," she whispered into the wind. "You believed in me all along."

She walked down the cobbled pathway alone. The spring leaves rustled as she passed them.